THE WAY TO HANITA

I read *The Way to Hanita* from beginning to end yesterday. It is a remarkable book, dealing with some of our most important national problems in an impressive and unique manner. It represents a fresh and vivid outlook on the holocaust, our Jewish heritage, and relations between Jews and Arabs in Israel.

You are to be congratulated on your clear and moving descriptions of the heartbreaking lives of Gerda and Rachel, which represent in many ways the lives of many of our immigrants as well as old-timers.

Your book should be read by Jews wherever they are, in order to broaden their understanding of the life and problems of the Jewish people both as individuals and a nation.

Ephraim Katzir
Fourth President of Israel

THE WAY TO HANITA

MYRA KAYE

MINERVA PRESS
MONTREUX LONDON WASHINGTON

THE WAY TO HANITA
Copyright © Myra Kaye 1995

All Rights Reserved

No part of this book may be reproduced in any form,
by photocopying or by any electronic or mechanical means,
including information storage or retrieval systems,
without permission in writing from both the copyright owner
and the publisher of this book.

ISBN 1 85863 716 3

First Published 1995 by
MINERVA PRESS
195 Knightsbridge
London SW7 1RE

2nd Impression 1996
3rd Impression 1997

Printed in Great Britain by
Antony Rowe Ltd, Chippenham, Wiltshire.

THE WAY TO HANITA

The Way to Hanita is now available in a Hebrew translation.

About the Author

Myra Kaye was born in Edinburgh, Scotland and studied Physics at Edinburgh and Cambridge Universities. After working in atomic research at AERE Hanwell, she moved to Israel, becoming Head of the Information Department and Library at the Soreq Nuclear Research Center. A noted science writer and editor and co-director of an International Course on Scientific Writing, she now devotes her time to writing fiction.

"And who knows if it is not the rivers of their tears
That have supported us. And brought us here.
And with their lives redeemed us all from God
And with their deaths assured us all of life
Eternal Life!"

Chaim Nachman Bialik

(Translated from the Hebrew by Misha Louvish)

All the world is a very narrow bridge;
What matters is, not to be afraid.

Rabbi Nachman of Breslau

(Translated from the Hebrew)

Acknowledgements

Many people helped me with this book, providing useful and constructive criticism and pointing out anachronisms or other errors. Some helped me by their lives, for while all the characters in *The Way to Hanita* are fictional, some of the events did happen to people I knew, most of whom are no longer alive. But, above all, I am grateful to my husband, Al Kaye, who took time from his scientific pursuits to give me valuable literary criticism and technical assistance, and who encouraged my belief that I had to write this book.

Lastly, I owe a debt of gratitude to Minerva Press and its fine staff for their expert handling of the manuscript.

For my son, David Kaye (1959-1979)

1. ISRAEL, 1978

I was working late at the office because we all take turns in filling in the Wednesday late night shift, 6-8pm, especially designed for those of the public who were working during the day and couldn't attend at our regular reception hours. You might find it puzzling why anyone who had a job needed the help of the Welfare Service, unless you knew the local conditions. Minimum wage for unskilled labour is equivalent to 350 dollars per month, not even enough to feed your average welfare family; that is, probably mother, father and nine kids, and a couple of 'dependent relatives' - a grandmother, the family moron, an unmarried aunt and so on. Nevertheless, not many came to what was obviously and tritely called the 'graveyard shift' - they preferred to take time off from work, which was always readily granted because everyone was involved in the national pastime, going to a government office to try and disentangle some bureaucratic snarl or get some licence or permit - and bosses were very understanding. Our clients preferred to sit around for two hours in the morning, waiting their turn, to getting something accomplished in ten minutes of their 'own' time. Naturally.

I was not alone. A security guard sat in the passage. Too many social workers had been threatened or actually injured by their sulky, abusive clients who felt they were getting a raw deal. One of my colleagues had been beaten up only a few months ago and then we got Yossi. After, of course, we had threatened to go on strike.

It was just as well. Only my second time on duty, a burly Napoleonesque-type walked into my room, sat down, and, as a preliminary to setting the rules of the game, took out from under his coat a large plastic bag, and from this, a knife, which he laid on the table between us. It wasn't one of those slender switch blade ones, which I understand can be deadly but look delicate and innocuous. This blade was about ten inches long and two inches wide. Even the handle was enormous. It looked like the knife a butcher would use for hacking through meat; camel meat, sinews and bones included.

Being new on the job, I swiftly did what I was supposed to do; smiled sweetly and pressed hard on the hidden button under my desk.

A couple of seconds later there was a polite, unalarming knock on the door, and Yossi came in.

"Excuse me Gerda, but do you have...?" by which time, having moved at something like the rate of a panther coming in for the kill, the knife was flying onto the floor behind him and he had Napoleon by the neck of his collar standing against the wall.

After he had frisked him, he picked up the knife.

"If I ever see anything like this on you again, I'll use it to cut off your balls," he said, dead quiet.

"Is there anything you want from this young lady?"

A shake of the head.

"Then I'll just show you out, SIR," upon which Yossi frog-marched him to the elevator and saw him to the door.

Security guards here are mostly ex-paratroopers. I wouldn't want to mix with them. They know all the tricks and when to use them.

This night, it was nearly eight o'clock. I had dealt with half a dozen people and helped them fill in the right forms and I was trying to decide whether I really ought to have a decent meal at a restaurant or just go straight home and fix myself a sandwich as usual, when there was a knock at the door. I had my head down, shuffling the forms into some sort of coherent order, so I didn't see her until she was sitting opposite me.

Most of our clients are what we call 'Easterners' - Jews from the Arab countries. Welfare applicants are the poor, the uneducated, the illiterate, the shiftless, men who came from countries where only women worked, countries where work was mostly primitive; a work ethic, a social conscience, unknown concepts. As Jews, they had been mercilessly persecuted and they have no love of government or authority. If I couldn't give them what they wanted, they almost invariably cursed this rotten country where the Western Jews had all the top jobs, and kept them down, and they threatened to leave - for Los Angeles, mostly - and I fervently hoped they would, but only a few of them did. The women were just as difficult - in fact the only difference was that instead of shouting and banging the table, they screeched and howled and wept.

As you might guess, I didn't like my job. Not that I blamed the 'Easterners' or looked down on them. They had a legitimate complaint. They had been put into an environment that held no niche for them.

This woman was an Ashkenazi - that is, she was of Western origin, probably European: pale skin, grey eyes, hair mostly white but still showing some of the original brown. She was not very well dressed - in fact she was poorly dressed. I thought I knew her type.

They were descendants, these Ashkenazi women, of the early pioneers who had died, while still young, of that deadly combination of malaria, overwork and malnutrition, or who were killed in the War of Independence. Mostly, poor innocents, thanking God for the opportunity to die for their country. The people who came on the Second Aliya, the wave of immigrants who came here at the turn of the century, mainly from Russia, were like that.

The widows went out to work, or took in sewing and managed somehow to bring up the children, but when the kids were grown up, or got killed in later wars or went off, or just didn't care - as happened, not too often, but it happened - these women were destitute. Nobody wanted sewing ladies these days. Everything came off the shelf. Two-dollar T-shirts from Taiwan, that spoke to you. Only today I had stood close to one that asked, "Feel like fucking?" Some had pictures of pop singers with their names spelled the way they sounded to the Taiwanese. Not even brides had hand-embroidered, initialled linen any more - they wanted quick-dry ready made synthetics. My mother had known and used sewing women. I didn't know any at all.

"Name please?" I asked, very politely. Such women were deeply ashamed, far too proud to seek charity until the last possible moment. A harsh look, and they fled.

She answered, and I began writing mechanically and then stopped. The family name was Arabic. So also was the accent. In fact so Arabic I could hardly comprehend what she was saying.

She was no relict of the Second Aliya.

Born?

Leipzig.

Date?

Fourth of July, 1930.

There was a distinct German pronunciation of 'Leipzig', but everything else was still pure Arabic, harsh and guttural; at any rate to Western ears.

"Married?"

"Not now."

I realised that when I came to the questions that needed more than one or two word answers I'd never be able to understand her. Quite apart from the awful distortion of the words, I had a feeling her Hebrew wasn't very good.

"Do you speak English?" (in English).

She understood, and shook her head. "Only a little."

"German?"

"Yes, I speak German," (more understandable, just a trace of the Arabic singsong). So we switched to German, which I simultaneously translated into Hebrew on the form.

I understand German because my father was a Berliner, at least, he studied law there but had the admirable good sense to leave in 1937, just one year short of his law degree, and come to Palestine. Here he met my English mother, who was visiting her cousin in Jerusalem and fell head over heels in love with this gentle, quiet man. She told me once that she first realised she loved him when a bus driver asked him if he had any small change, and he replied, "I have *only* small change". I came to the next question.

"Religion?" I asked.

She hesitated for a moment, then extended her hand and drew up her sleeve. I never get over seeing the numbers tattooed on the wrist. I heard a man in a BBC talk programme once say that it wasn't really a good idea to find and prosecute Nazi war criminals hiding in Britain, "because the Holocaust happened so long ago it is no longer relevant to us; and that those people should not be punished, their conscience was their punishment."

Here, the Holocaust existed around us, also within us. We had passed it on to our children, too, without conscious volition, because it was a part of what we were.

Consciences? They didn't have them. They were proud of their Nazi past, they would have loved to have it all over again, to have it go on forever. All this floated briefly through my mind as I wrote down "Jewish".

"Do you have somewhere to stay?"

"No."

"Any money?"

"I have twenty lirot."

That isn't much, about ten dollars. None of them have much.

"Where did you stay last night?"

"At the hospital."

"Were you sick? Which hospital?"

"The city hospital. In Hebron. I worked there. As a cleaner."

This was a complication. Hebron was on the Occupied West Bank. It had a Military Government, but the internal affairs of Hebron would be run by an urban Municipal Council.

"Why did you leave?"

"They sent me away."

"Why?"

"Because I was Jewish."

"How long did you work there?"

"Twenty years."

That made it since 1958, when Hebron was under Jordanian rule.

"Are you a Jordanian citizen? Do you have a Jordanian passport?"

A shrug of the shoulders. "No. No citizenship, no passport."

But because she was so obviously Jewish, according to the Law of Return, she would only have to go through the bare formalities at the Interior Ministry office before they gave her an identity card as an Israeli citizen - and a passport if she wanted it.

"Why didn't you go to the Hebron Municipality? If you worked there so long you must have had some rights? Severance pay, for instance?"

"They wouldn't talk to me. They sent me to the Military Government. They said they couldn't deal with my case as I was 'a foreigner'."

"What happened there?"

"The Military Governor said local problems like this weren't his business. He told me to go to the Municipality. I told him I had been there and they had sent me to him. A captain gave me twenty lirot and told me to come here. He wrote down the address."

"Did he authorise the twenty lirot from some fund?"

"No, he took it out of his wallet. He got me a lift on a jeep."

"You came straight here?"

"Yes."

I looked up at her again, and found myself gazing straight into her eyes. They were grey, very direct and very beautiful. The rest of her face was too old, too knocked about by time to be beautiful, but her eyes were. She must have been a stunner when she was young. No wonder the captain gave her twenty lirot.

I said, "The problem is, your case is complicated. You haven't been living in Israel. I can't really help you till we get your citizenship straightened out. That will take a little time. I suggest you come back here tomorrow. It's too late now. Tomorrow we can talk to the various authorities."

I paused for a moment.

"Come back here at ten o'clock tomorrow morning, when I start." (Late, because of the Wednesday night duty.) "Don't wait in the queue. Come straight to this room. I'll tell the guard. My name is Gerda. Ask for me."

This was strictly out of order. We all took our clients anonymously, according to a number system, first come, first served, otherwise there was mayhem. I didn't consider why I did this. She thanked me, and I rose to go.

"One minute," I said, "We have to get you settled for the night." We didn't have to, and often we couldn't and didn't, but I wanted to, in her case.

"There is a cheap hotel. It's fairly clean, not very clean; it mostly has young Arabs from Gaza who work in Israel and stay there overnight. (This was also illegal, but, since it suited everybody at the time, the police turned a blind eye). It's very cheap. You can get a room for ten lirot."

"No."

Puzzled. "The only other place is a sort of hostel, mainly for hippie-type kids from abroad. They usually play their radios half the night and kick up a hell of a noise. It's not any cleaner and it would cost you more; fifteen lirot. Would that be all right?"

She said, "Yes. That would be all right."

I gave her the address and the number of the bus that would get her there.

Idly I asked her, "Do you have a Jewish name?" It wasn't one of the questions on the form. I just wanted to know, for myself.

"Just 'Rachel'."

"You have to eat, too, so I'm going to give you twenty lirot from our emergency fund which should see you over until breakfast tomorrow."

We did have such a fund but we only used it for the most dire cases, men and women who had hardly eaten for days, women who had babies, or lots of young children, people who virtually couldn't survive another day without help. It was a small fund, and the authorities didn't like it because we had the powers of decision over its allocation, not them, so it was paid into weekly to keep us under supervision. We called it the Slush Fund, and by Wednesday evening it was more slush than fund. I opened the tin box, and there was only one ten lira note in it, so I turned my back on Rachel and surreptitiously added another from my handbag. I made her sign a receipt and hoped she wouldn't notice it was only for ten lirot. She was supposed to return it when she was able. Hardly anybody ever did.

The trouble with Rachel, I thought gloomily, was she didn't fit into any category. If she was a battered wife, there was a shelter; a drug addict, there was a hostel; if she were sick I could send her to a hospital. But she wasn't any of these. She was just homeless and poor. "No family?" I said automatically. I was already standing up, preparatory to leaving.

"I have two daughters."

"Are either of them in Israel?"

"One lives in Jerusalem."

"Couldn't she help you?"

"No."

I had been very close to my mother, my loving mother who had tried so hard to muddle her way into my problems, without understanding them at all, but who had helped so much just by being there for me. So I did not understand this. Rachel had spoken in a simple conversational way, as if it hardly mattered to her at all. On impulse, I said, "I've got to eat, too. Let's eat together, then I'll drive you over to the hostel." She looked doubtful, and this made me more determined. "Put your coat on," I said, forgetting she hadn't any. So she lifted up her plastic bag and followed me to the door.

Fraternising with the clients is strictly forbidden, under a direct and specific edict. This is not because of incipient favouritism, but to protect us from very real danger. Some years ago, one of our social workers took pity on a sixteen-year-old kid who had been thrown out of his home by a father who drank, watched indifferently by a mother who had eight other kids and the spirit long knocked out of her. She offered to put him up for a night or two until he got sorted out. It turned out he was on heroin, he stole all her more valuable possessions and sold them to pay for drugs, and he refused to get out of her apartment. If she forced him to leave, he said he would say that she had raped him. Fortunately, she was strong-minded, she got a burly friend to kick him out and when he did scream "rape", there was a half-hearted police investigation, but nobody believed him. Nevertheless, our supervisor made it clear that taking a client to your home was absolutely forbidden, as was any show of 'personal interest'. I thought taking Rachel for a meal probably did come under 'personal interest', but I was going to do it all the same. So few things did interest me. I lived in a woolly cloud of other people's problems. I was drab. I looked and felt drab. But Rachel interested me. On the way out she paused and asked:

"Do you think you will be able to do something for me?"

Actually, the numbers on her wrist were like money in the bank. No one at the Ministry of the Interior was going to make a big fuss and start time-consuming queries as to whether she was really Jewish. She'd sail through the formalities in no time and come out with her citizenship and identity card. She could be eligible for welfare benefits and maybe even some kind of social security pension and last, but certainly not least, she might be entitled to reparations from the German government who couldn't give you back your parents or your spouse or your children, but at least compensation for the plunder, the family silver, the house, the well-beloved furniture, your relatives' gold teeth and hair. Given time, I could probably make her reasonably comfortable. So I said reassuringly,

"Yes, but it will take a little time. Be patient."

She smiled. Her smile was as beautiful as her eyes. "I'm patient," she said.

Going out, Yossi stopped us. You aren't allowed to go out with a client in case he (she) is secretly holding you at gun or knife point.

I explained to Yossi that it was OK, and he listened and then said to Rachel, "You can go down first." She didn't understand, so I told her in German and asked her to wait for me outside, it was a rule, and she went.

"It wasn't necessary." I said crossly to Yossi, and he just smiled and held on to my arm. The Army trains them thoroughly.

Rachel, to my relief, was waiting for me in the street. I could not explain to myself, at that point, nor that much better even later, why she mattered to me. I had been taught, and I had learned well, not to get emotionally involved with any clients. Some of them, even most of them, were in a far worse state than Rachel: the battered wives with bruised faces, dazed eyes and clinging, crying children; cancer victims with no place to die; men and women and children who had been abandoned by cruelty, by chance, by the vagaries of life, by the death of a partner. Unlucky people, lonely people, the stupid and the incapable, the handicapped, by birth, or by accident, or the savagery of man.

We got them all. Not the war invalids, of course; the Army looked after its own. But all the others streamed past my desk and of course I had become hardened, I had to, or I couldn't do my job.

Many of them looked more appealing than Rachel, some of them were tragic and beautiful even, yet I managed to listen to them, and sift out their stories into the mostly irrelevant facts that went into the forms, without feeling the urge to intervene in such a personal way. Sometimes I gave a client a few lirot from my pocket to meet some urgent, individual need. Not enough money to be important, and not enough caring for me to remember the face. Conscience money, almost immediately forgotten. So, surprised at myself, I took Rachel by the arm and led her to my car, which was an eighteen-year-old VW Beetle - more repair than car.

She looked at it, and said, "No!" She volunteered no explanation. "Claustrophobia?" I wondered. But it wasn't that. Was it because it was a German car? So we walked. It wasn't far, and it was in the direction of the hostel.

We went to Hamozeg, of course. In the last ten years or so, the restaurant face of Tel Aviv has changed from restaurants offering mid-European fare, schnitzels made of turkey and beef stews made of gristle, and middle Eastern restaurants serving humus and tehina and shislik and kebab, plus a few speciality restaurants, strictly for tourists only, or those earning tourist salaries.

Since then, Tel Aviv has acquired Beautiful People, and, with them, a huge variety of ethnic-style restaurants, Chinese and Thai, Indian restaurants with authentic tandoori and curries; home-made Italian pasta; French pâtés and sauces; you could have it all.

The old-timers, however, who went out to eat, not to dine, still mostly went to Hamozeg. It had been there since before the beginning of the State. It was a small chain of three or four restaurants, and they all looked alike, with the heavy dark wood and faded plush of the '30s.

Most people who ate there ate alone, lived alone, and they nearly all ordered the goulash soup.

Hamozeg served a full menu, the schnitzel and the like, at reasonable prices, but the goulash soup was special. For about half the price of a 'real' meat dish, you got a full soup plate, the old-fashioned kind with a well in the centre, not a bowl, brimming to the top with what was really a thin stew, rich in meat and potatoes, mostly, sometimes carrots and peas, or other vegetables, and with a hunk of good Israeli black bread to mop it up with, it was usually enough to satisfy the most ravenous appetite. You almost always finished it, because it was delicious, and, if you were greedy, you ended up with a pastry (they were also enormous at Hamozeg, yeast cakes as eaten "In der Heim") and a cup of coffee, and then you could stagger out into the coldest weather and not feel a thing.

So I took Rachel to the nearest Hamozeg. She sat down and stared around her.

"What's wrong? Is something the matter?" I was wary.

"No."

"What is it you find so interesting? It's just a restaurant."

"I've never been in a real restaurant before. Just cafés."

I handed her a menu and explained to her, in German, what everything was. She looked at me helplessly and shrugged. Yet her eyes were terribly excited, like those of a young girl at her first grown-up party. Perhaps it was these contrasts in Rachel that intrigued me. I couldn't figure her out.

I ordered, of course, the goulash soup for both of us. She ate in a peculiar way. She was obviously very hungry, yet she ate very slowly, chewing each piece many times. She did not raise her eyes from her plate, and when she was finished, I saw her take a piece of bread and put it in her pocket. She did this secretly yet automatically. I was not, however, surprised. I had seen this happen with people from the Camps before. I tried to get her to talk about herself, but she was very unresponsive and answered me mostly in monosyllables. She did not initiate any conversation.

Although it was obvious she had great natural reserve, I guessed also that eating was something she did with total concentration. She was also probably very tired.

So I left her alone, and, in a silence that was not uncomfortable, I paid the bill, and put her on a bus. She thanked me and I walked back to my car with a feeling in me that puzzled me, not because it was complex or unfamiliar, but because it was out of context. After a time I recognised it. When I moved away from home, my mother used to come to visit me and we often went out for a coffee or a meal. It was that feeling: of separation, but also trust and love.

I don't usually get to the office much before nine even on ordinary days, although officially we open at eight. But like most of the others, I usually work far more than the hours required of me, and the office supervisor is understanding and only scolds occasionally.

But this time I was there practically on the dot of nine, despite the two hours owing to me from the "graveyard shift". I combed my hair and put on some lipstick and put up a notice, "Back soon", on my door and went to see the Head, who is the Head of the whole outfit in Tel Aviv, not just Supervisor of our office. Dr Lustig: very high-up in the hierarchy.

I liked him immensely. One of the things I liked about him was that he always has time for each one of us, you never had to "make an appointment" and then wait till whatever it was you had wanted was no longer important, or practical, or you had lost that first fresh enthusiasm that could make you persuasive and make your point. So I knocked on the door and went in, and he said:

"Hi Gerda! You look terrific. What can I do for you?"

He is a "Yekke", i.e. of German origin, speaks Hebrew with a German accent, dresses very properly and has an extremely sober, intelligent face, with humour only just lurking behind his eyes.

"I want some money from the Special Fund. I have a new case. A woman."

"Under what category does she qualify?"

There was no way out of this one, so I said, "I don't know. Can we find a way? She's a Holocaust survivor."

He just looked at me. He didn't need to say anything. I had seen the numbers tattooed also on his wrist, under the clean white cuff. You found them everywhere, and in the most unexpected places. On the wrist of a Cabinet Minister cutting a ribbon for a new highway, a garbage collector lifting up your garbage bin. If that were a qualification, the Special Fund would have had to be about as big as the budget of the Ministry itself.

An explanation about the Special Fund.

2 ISRAEL, 1973

The Special Fund arose as a result of a brilliant piece of investigative reporting carried out by a local newspaper man early in the 1970's. This enterprising young journalist's curiosity was piqued by a colleague's remark that there were probably about a hundred Righteous Gentiles in Israel, a great many of them living in conditions of extreme poverty.

'Righteous Gentiles' is the name given to those non-Jews who, during World War II, across the continent of Europe, sheltered Jews from the Nazi death machine, almost always at the risk of their own lives. Some of them hid their husbands or lovers, some took in the child of a Jewish friend. Others sheltered people entirely unknown to them, Jews fleeing from the big cities into the only sometimes safer remote villages where they might find a farmer with a hayloft, a peasant with a cellar. A whole Protestant village in France hid literally hundreds of Jews, doubling its population every few weeks as each lot was sent over the border to Switzerland, and although most of them were caught and sent back, a fair number did make it to safety.

The Righteous Gentiles are cherished, not only by the people whose lives they saved and their families, but also they are nationally cherished. At the Holocaust Memorial, the Ultimate Memorial that was built in Jerusalem, an avenue of trees leads up to the stark hall where every flagstone bears the name of a Camp and in the centre burns an eternal flame. Each tree has been planted in the name of a Righteous Gentile. There are not very many of them. During the years, they visit here, attend their tree-planting ceremony, still head-scarved peasants or urbane Berliners, little old Frenchwomen. All kinds of people. Brave people, or caring people, rigid with justified pride. Then they leave to go back to their own lives.

Coming out of the Holocaust Museum (you could make a fortune selling Kleenex to hardened politicians on official visits; American ladies in plastic trouser suits with tin jewellery and Shirley Temple hair; Sabras born at not twenty minutes walking distance, to whom Europe was only a name; Moroccan Jews; Japanese gentiles - no-one leaves the Yad Vashem Holocaust Memorial with dry eyes) - coming out, you passed between these cool vibrant trees. It was there you thought of the Righteous Gentiles, a bridge to the living world.

The Righteous Gentiles are now mostly elderly and the bright young Israeli reporter with a video camera captured the daily lives of a few of them that had settled here.

An old man, once a small-time farmer in Poland, in his bare room, with an iron bed and a rectangular sink filled with glass milk bottles (sterilised milk seemed to be his preference - fresh milk comes in plastic bags). A loaf of bread. An oil stove with a kettle on it; a dirty cup. Trousers drying on the back of a chair, a checked shirt, a workman's cap. Sullen suspiciousness of the very old and poor, almost no Hebrew, a little Yiddish, his Jewish wife dead these past five years. A few hundred lirot a month from the Welfare Ministry at best, or charity from friends.

Another, a woman this time, also solitary but much neater, 'the family' (meaning the child she had saved, now himself a father) were on Welfare, but tried to help out. Still very basic. An old refrigerator with a bowl of apples and a plate of blintzes. Crude red cotton curtains on the window. The same Jewish Agency issue metal frame bed, with the original mattress, made in three pieces and filled with straw. Bright, perky, sociable, but still too near the breadline, and very old and deaf. The family visited every day but there didn't seem much they could do. And so on.

The reporter gleefully collected half a dozen of these living portraits, selected three, added an indignant commentary and a recitative, (to the extent he could extract information), on who these people were and what they had done to make them Righteous. He added his by-line and gave the tape to the editor of the weekly TV consumers' programme.

It was presented to the nation, with the addition of a single simple question: "What was the Government going to do about it?"

The Government didn't have any choice. The nation rose with an almighty roar. An indignant public dragged the Minister of the Interior from his bed and called him a monster. The phones at his Ministry, as well as in his home, never ceased to ring. The Prime Minister was also given a hard time, and came down in his fury on the Interior Minister too, and the Treasury Minister for good measure.

In a country never known for the swiftness of its legislation, in which vital laws on environmental protection, electoral reform, civil liberties, languish for years at the Committee stage, where nitpickers pick nits out of them, the Righteous Gentile Pension Law (hardly seeing a Committee in passing) was drafted and went through the Knesseth (unanimously, of course) in only six days. They got generous allowances for life. Meanwhile, the Housing Minister, only recently excoriated because he could not provide one apartment for a polio-paralysed mother of three, magically produced enough three-room apartments, in the best districts of whatever towns they inhabited, for the Righteous Gentiles, and moved them in at once, together with basic furnishings (including of course, a TV set) purchased by yet more miraculous money from the bankrupt Ministry of Immigrant Absorption.

These bewildered people became society's darlings. The best hotels made them luncheon parties, fetching them from their new homes in especially rented buses. The Tourist Bureau took them on free trips round the country, wherever they wanted to go.

As a cynical social worker, I was sure that we had most likely succeeded, by making them financially secure, also in taking away some of their purpose in life.

They were left without anything to strive for, without the daily treasure hunt which might turn up, somewhere, a worn but still serviceable blanket, a cast out sofa, a stove that worked. What joy!

I am not knocking comfort or security, especially for the old. But it is a fact that many of them drifted back from the neat three-room flats with the television sets in the well-kept apartment houses full of people who spoke, incomprehensibly, only Hebrew, and had names like Ma'ayan or Meirav and Stav. They returned to the old neighbourhoods, to live again, this time like slightly better off poor people, among other people who also had always been poor, and spoke Polish, or Romanian, which they could understand. And had proper names, like 'Yankele' and 'Yossele' and 'Channele'. They added a few luxuries; a plate or two, a comfortable chair, an electric heater even, or a radio; they ate margarine and jam with their bread and there was always tea. The monthly cheques went, largely untouched, into the bank accounts.

The Welfare Ministry appointed a special Social Worker to keep an eye on them. Occasionally, someone needed a nurse for a time, or fancied a hot meal. She was kept busy. But these were mostly people who had always lived simple, obscure lives, and had got used to it, and wanted to go on that way in the pride of their independence until they died. In the midst of all this flutter, the Minister, frightened, dreamed up the Special Fund. It was for fish that got out of the net.

Israel, because of the unnatural length and severity of its birth pangs, is more than usually generously endowed with unsung heroes. Poets who lived on air and poetry when even a working man had little bread. Lunatics who insisted on speaking Hebrew, which nobody knew in their time and who, by sheer obstinacy, got the national tongue going. Youngsters who parachuted into the Camps to tell the dying Jews there was hope (there was no hope) and some of whom lived and returned to tell the tale. Directors who put on plays with no actors and no stage. Those who organised the illegal immigration of walking tragedies, people like Rachel and worse; a Government out of people who had never governed; an army out of people who had never fought. Exploits that could never be told.

Most of these people, now oldsters, were caught up in various nets. The Mossad, like the Army, looked after its own. Anyone who had worked ten years in a job he could talk about, had Social Security. But there were some fish that slipped out. Actors who had built the National Theatre. Painters. Writers. Educators. Civilians who had carried out still untellable, hard and heroic exploits. And their relicts and dependants.

The Minister of the Interior, badly burned, or, in a perhaps more appropriate idiom, having been caught more or less literally with his trousers down, called the Head of the Welfare Dept., our Dr Lustig, promptly to his office and told him that if ever an item appeared in the news, whether press, radio or television, or even someone's autobiography, that even hinted that someone who had served the State well had not been taken care of by that same State in his old age and/or poverty, he (the Minister) would have his (Dr Lustig's) balls. Being a religious man, he probably didn't use these words, but that was the gist of it.

He then told Dr Lustig about the Fund.

"How much?" Dr Lustig, ever the practical, asked.

"As much as it takes."

"On what basis? For what needs?"

"Whatever you think."

"To whom am I accountable?"

The Minister then told him he was accountable only to him personally, added another few threats on much the same lines as before, and opened the door. Dr Lustig exited, bewildered, and went off for four days to a Kibbutz Guest House where, after pacing the soothing shores of Lake Kinneret for four hours, wrote voluminous notes that were afterwards sorted out into an eight-page booklet entitled "Guidelines to the Use of the Special Fund". The booklets were distributed to the social workers in the Welfare Departments. There was only one guideline that was at all useful - the last one - that said firmly that monies from the Special Fund could not be used without the specific authorisation of Dr Lustig personally. Of course, the news got around and, at first, we were flooded with applications, some ludicrous, some merely greedy, some impudent.

I had a 'client', for instance, who demanded lifetime support from the Special Fund because he had done the country a favour in coming to it at all, and giving up the joys of life in a Syrian village. Another claimed to have cured a vast section of the population of headaches and back pains by the laying on of hands, which, however, caused such a drain on his vital energies that he was unable to work... And so on. Poor Dr Lustig sat up patiently into the night, carefully weighing up all this rubbish before setting down his stamp of disapproval.

I did get one real case though, and it was interesting.

Tall, pale, willowy figure; would bend in any decent gale. Sad eyes, quiet voice and cultured Hebrew, about sixty I would guess. A lady. A lady fallen on hard times. Handbag, leather, scuffed but polished; shoes too. A very proper light coat, with all the buttons in place. The sad eyes were also dull eyes. Suffering, but not a fighter. A lonely woman.

"Name?" I asked.

"Anna."

"Anna what - family name, please?"

"Just Anna."

I let it go. I put my forms "Application for Welfare", plus supplements I-VI, to the side, and said, "What's the story?"

The story was that she had been a widow for about two years already. She had not seen her husband for a long time; he worked abroad, for the Mossad. He had died in Paris while she was on her way to join him for a few days. This was where they usually met, once or twice a year - it was too dangerous for him to come to Israel. He had been killed in a bus accident. It was apparently not connected with his work, just an accident, one of five casualties; all perfectly ordinary people.

The Mossad had notified her, and he had been buried in Paris. Someone had gone with her and then brought her back. The allowances she got as a wife had stopped and she was not getting her widow's pension.

From my questioning, I learned that this sort of life had been going on for a long time. She had been married thirty years ago, and after a brief year together he had gone off, leaving her in this limbo of twice a year; at best, a couple of days together, and then silence. She never knew when, either. A Mossad man would call on her and one day later she would be on the plane. I understood that her husband had been a "sleeper" in one of the Arab countries, probably Iraq. I was a bit surprised, because family men do not usually get these long term, virtually life-time assignments. They don't accept them.

I said to her, "You should be getting your widow's pension from Mossad. Why don't you apply to them?"

"Mossad's the problem. I've applied. I've talked to them a dozen times. I don't get straight answers - 'We're looking into it, Anna, in the meantime here's a cheque...' I can't live like that! I have a feeling there's something they won't tell me."

I said I'd talk to them and I arranged a meeting with my contact person in Mossad. She was right. Mossad, of course, paid its widows generous pensions. The problem was, in this case, that there were two; my widow and a widow in Baghdad with six kids. The Mossad's Financial Head, not known for his flexibility, and smarting under a recent accusation in the Knesset Finance Committee that Mossad spent money like it was always Christmas, baulked at paying two widow's pensions. After bitter arguments, he announced that he was going to pay the widow in Baghdad because she had the six kids and because she had actually been living with the fellow for these last twenty-five years. He wasn't going to pay anyone else - one agent, one pension. "I'm a reasonable man," he said. (He was not) "But what if one of these fucking idiots becomes an undercover Moslem? Would I have to pay four fucking pensions to all his fucking wives? How would that look on the books? It would look as if I was fiddling, that's how it would look!" Whether there had been a divorce of my lady, or whether there had been a valid re-marriage, nobody knew and nobody was going to ask questions in Baghdad, or elsewhere. The decision, therefore, was purely pragmatic.

The Iraqi lady got a letter from Buenos Aires from an extremely respectable legal firm announcing that her husband's business assets in Argentina had been consolidated and invested in gilt-edged securities (list attached) that would provide her with a monthly income (of whatever sum Mossad thought she would need). A first cheque was enclosed and they would be at her service at any time. The Mossad prided itself on its laundering service. You might be able to trace Mafia money if you set aside a few years to do it, but Mossad money - never.

After I got this information, I wrote it all up as an application for a widow's pension, at Mossad's going rates, to be paid from the Special Fund.

Dr Lustig's beaming approval came promptly and by hand the following day. We arranged payment through Mossad so that she would never know and I am told she goes every year to Paris to lay flowers on his unfaithful grave.

Truthfully, I couldn't see any reason that would qualify Rachel to be a beneficiary of the Special Fund. But I had such a great belief in her that I asked Dr Lustig:

"Will you at least see her? Speak to her personally?"

"If you want me to." A pause. A long pause. Then: "Get her to fill in a work application form." Dr Lustig never does anything without a reason, so this gave me a glimmer of hope.

3 ISRAEL, 1978

When I got back to my office, Rachel was already there. There was the usual, I suppose justified, yelling outside my door. "She jumped the queue", "Why should she get in first?" "I've got three kids waiting for me at home", and, of course, bitterly, "Ashkenazi!"

I said to Rachel, "How are you? Did you have a good night? You look rested, I guess you must have!" Rachel indeed looked blooming. She wore the same nondescript, elderly, printed cotton dress which presumably was all she had, she carried the same plastic bag, but there was something about her posture, a shiny look in her eyes, that made her seem ten years younger.

"Actually I hardly slept at all. The kids were having a farewell party for one of the girls who was going home to New York. In one of the rooms, it was opposite mine, they invited me in. I wouldn't have been able to sleep anyway - two guitars, a banjo and a ukulele! I liked them so much, they were nice kids. Young people are so lovely."

I said stupidly, "I guess it must have taken you back to the days of your youth."

"I never had any youth."

The old Rachel was back. Silent. Reserved. Older.

"I've got some forms I'm going to help you fill in. After that, I'm going to introduce you to the Head of the Department who might be able to help you more than I can. The trouble is, everything's so slow. I'll give you some papers which you have to take to the Registration Department of the Ministry of the Interior. They'll send you (where?) an identity card in a few days, that goes fast, and of course you'll get automatic citizenship under the Law of Return, but then everything else takes simply ages. Compensation from Germany, for example, there's a complication: you're from what's East Germany now..."

Rachel interrupted. "No," she said.

"You're not from Leipzig?"

"I don't want compensation from Germany."

"You're making a mistake. It's an income for life. It's security and they owe it to you. Without what they did, a woman like you, you'd have a profession."

Rachel said, "They gave me a profession."

I looked at her doubtfully. "You said you did cleaning."

"They taught me whoring. I was the best whore in the Camp."

I did not look at her but silently picked up the employment form, read out the questions in German, and wrote down her replies in Hebrew. For "work experience" she directed me to write "cleaning". I glanced at her then, and she was looking straight at me with her mocking smile.

I said, "How old were you when you got sent to a Camp?"

"Is that one of the questions?"

"You know it isn't."

"Then why do you want to know?"

I hesitated. This was something I had to work out. There were locked doors in my life, doors I needed to open in order to gain self-understanding, doors which I had locked against myself and thrown away the key. There was a connection I couldn't comprehend with the Holocaust, the Holocaust in all of us, as well as my own personal holocaust.

Why did I feel that Rachel was my key? She, alone, my only key?

So I didn't answer, and Rachel looked at me, looked at me for quite a long time, with those hard intelligent grey eyes, and I knew I was being judged and I begged silently, "Don't send me to the left, to the gas chamber, send me to the right, to life". I don't know to whom this strange request was addressed, not to a God to whom I gave no atom of credence; and surely not to the person that was Rachel.

As soon as I realised what I was thinking, I was appalled. It was melodrama. It was cheap. Sacrilegious, even. I wasn't the type. Yet it was not wrong; my life was drifting by me, I was not in my life. It was a matter of survival. I think she understood.

"I was sent to a military camp when I was thirteen. My parents were probably in Auschwitz. I was living with a cousin, she was a few years older than me. Probably my parents were dead, but I didn't know. The cousin was in hiding. She didn't wear the yellow star. She used to pass by her parents, her brothers and sisters on the street, without a word. Once, when an SS officer was looking, she spat at her sister and called her a "dirty Jew".

It didn't help her. It didn't help either of us. We were sent to an SS training camp as Army whores."

"Wasn't it an offence to sleep with a Jewish woman?"

"We weren't women. We were whores."

I didn't want to press her, so I waited. She went on:

"My cousin didn't last long. She wasn't as pretty as I was. She became an enlisted man's whore. She got gonorrhoea almost immediately and they shot her. But anyway, she wouldn't have lasted more than a couple of years. I was special - a thirteen-year-old virgin! So I got to be an officer's whore. That meant I could last four years, maybe even five, before they got rid of me.

"But I was a clever whore. I went after a colonel, an elderly man, I got him mad for me, I learnt from the others how to please him. I used to lie with men on top of me, inventing new tricks, and it worked. After a time he took me into his quarters for his own private use. I would live as long as he liked me. I thought I would live forever. What's the next question?"

"I'm sorry?"

"The next question. On the form."

So we completed all the forms and I called Dr Lustig and he said I could bring her up now. We went out, I hung up the "Back soon" notice on my door and we walked along the corridor and climbed the stairs to the accompaniment of mutters and screams in a variety of languages, all angry and none of them complimentary, from my waiting customers.

Dr Lustig may be genuinely kindly, but he's nobody's pushover. He asked us to sit down, gave me a perfunctory nod, then addressed himself exclusively to Rachel. He spoke in German, and he was nasty, probing every weak spot.

"I understand you need a job?"

"Yes."

"Do you have any professional qualifications?"

"No."

"Have you ever done any practical nursing?"

A slight hesitation. Then, firmly, "No."

"Do you speak Hebrew?"

"No."

"None at all? Could you run a household, do shopping for instance, in Hebrew?"

"Not in Hebrew."

All these questions were asked by a Dr Lustig looking piously at the ceiling, at the walls, moving papers on his desk. Now he quickly and suddenly stared straight at Rachel.

Her hands were resting on her lap: she was a picture of calm composure. Not a trace of the anxiety you might expect in a penniless woman seeing her only hope of a decent job fading away. Dr Lustig grunted.

He changed his direction and the questions became more personal; nevertheless they were presented in the most impersonal way possible, very distant, very polite.

"Could you look after a sick man?"

"Yes."

"Even if you knew he was dying? Can you look after a dying person? Can you cope with death?"

"Yes."

"How do you know?"

Rachel said, "I've had a lot of experience."

"The job I have in mind doesn't require Hebrew, but it's temporary, and others might. Are you willing to learn?"

"Yes."

"Can you cook?"

"Arab food."

"Do you have any dependants?"

"No."

"You wouldn't mind a full-time live-in job - of course there'd be help with night nursing when it is needed."

Rachel hesitated, for a long time. At last she said, "I'd want a room. My own room."

Dr Lustig exploded. "Well naturally, woman, of course you'll have your own room! This isn't an Escort Agency! This man is dying. He needs a nurse, not a concubine. For Christ's sake, he's sixty-six years old!"

"I know. I mean a room of my own, not in his house. A separate place."

"You aren't going to have much free time to be there." I noticed, gladly, that the grammatical tense had changed. Whatever the job was, apparently he was going to give her a shot at it.

"It doesn't matter."

"You still want it?"

"Yes."

"Would you take the job without it?"

"If it doesn't give me enough money to rent a room, no."

Dr Lustig didn't argue. He could have pointed out that she didn't have any alternatives, but what was the point? In a curious way, they were not employer and prospective employee - they were equals, bargaining over a service for a service, with mutual firmness, and mutual respect. Dr Lustig was sensitive enough to appreciate this, and I think he enjoyed it. He smiled, with irony, but also with genuine pleasure, and he said, "OK., Rachel, you've got it." His use of her first name was not patronising - in this country you are on first name terms with the President from the moment you become acquainted, even if you are only his garbage collector.

"I'll tell you about it. There's a gentleman, he's of German origin, speaks German - speaks Italian, French, English, Hebrew, Arabic also, just about anything you want for that matter - he's sixty-six, I told you that, no signs of senility - on the contrary, extremely intelligent; also extremely bad-tempered, opinionated, obstinate, sharp, rude, not to put too fine an edge on it, impossible to live with. He's got leukaemia, dying, maybe another six months to go, who knows, maybe even a year. He's in remission now, you'd never know it. But, any day - dizziness, weakness, headaches, fainting; then there's the chemotherapy. Tell me, Rachel, can you wipe up vomit?"

"Yes."

"And change sheets with pee on them, or worse, and feed a man with a spoon and wipe the dribble, and do all these things and still leave him his dignity, can you do all that?"

"Yes."

"I know, 'you've had experience'. He won't thank you, you know. He'll resent you like hell. Nothing you do will be good enough. He'll tell you you're clumsy and stupid. Because inside, though he'll never show it, he's very frightened. Can you understand this? Can you handle it?"

Rachel gave him her sweet smile. "As you say - I've had experience."

Dr Lustig said, "These are the terms. You'll get the standard salary of a practical nurse based on an eight-hour day, but you'll get extra for overtime and you'll be working a lot of overtime. Your employer will give you housekeeping money and I'm sure you'll have to account to him for every agora. We'll probably have to make other arrangements about that later. You'll earn more than enough for a room, live it up and get one with a kitchen and bath too.

"Professor Strumpfeld has his own terms. He's refused to go into a hospital. He won't go into a nursing home or an Old Age Home, sorry, Senior Citizen's Residence, he won't have a trained nurse looking after him, he won't live with his son, don't blame him, the chap's one of those religious fanatics. After a lot of yelling he's agreed to having what he calls a 'household help' on the condition that she does exactly what he tells her, never bothers him and doesn't talk unless she's spoken to. He'll try this for twenty-four hours, and if he doesn't like it, she has to go."

"He understands his state of health and the prognosis perfectly. He says when he's bedridden he'll think again, probably all he will want is a bottle of whiskey and to go off peacefully. Do you agree to all this nonsense?"

Rachel said, "It sounds perfectly sensible to me."

"Gerda will make the arrangements. You can start today. Can you do that?"

"Yes."

"Gerda, give her some money for clothes and things from the Special Fund, I'll sign for it."

He stood up and held out his hand. "Good luck," he said.

Rachel didn't thank him. She nodded when she shook his hand, but she didn't say anything. He liked that. Queen Nobody to the last. I was surprised he didn't bow to the waist and kiss her hand.

We went downstairs to my office, but the crowd howled so menacingly that I asked Rachel if she would mind waiting a little and took one of them in.

She told me a long tale of an unemployed husband and no bread for the children but she was wearing two gold chains and when I admired her ear-rings she assured me that the diamonds were real.

When we got down to business, it turned out there was only one kid at home, the others were all grown up, and working. Her husband had a disability pension for an ulcer, probably long healed, and he 'helped out a bit' at the open-air market, which meant he worked 'unofficially' - that is, without paying income tax - and earned a lot more than I did. I said we would look into it and she extended her hands which I now noticed had three gold rings and said "bread!" piteously and stalked out on new rather high-heeled shoes. "Hearts of stone," she addressed the crowd (there were ten of them), "Thank God we have good children, or we wouldn't even have even a video or a washing machine. No thanks to *them*, they don't even look after *their own*." (She meant Ashkenazis, of course.)

The next client was a man who was genuinely sick, genuinely unemployed. He had an invalid wife and two kids and another on the way, and a slipped disc. I wondered pruriently whether he had acquired it while making this third child, and if so, how; did his wife's disability require some strange and interesting position? I arranged to have him put on Welfare and explained to him about Sickness Benefits and promised to speak to the Sick Fund people about upping the priority on his operation because they needed him at home.

4 ISRAEL, GERMANY, ENGLAND, ITALY, 1915-1978

I went out after this and told Rachel to come with me. I didn't want to put her through running the gauntlet back into my own room, where I reckoned the situation was getting to be something like storming the Bastille. However, my clients had got to know each other in the interval, and were chatting together quite amicably, cursing their adopted country, and expressing the usual threats of leaving it for Los Angeles or New York.

There was no more than a menacing growl as I dashed out yet again with papers and a telephone directory and a propitiating, "I'll be back in ten minutes and I promise I'll see you all without delay."

I took Rachel into an empty office and started to get through the paperwork, which, because it pertained to the Special Fund, was far less than you might expect. I opened a file on Professor Strumpfeld, having ascertained, thankfully, from Dr Lustig's secretary that she hadn't done it yet - I wanted this file with me, I was already jealous. Rachel was mine.

I made out a cheque to Rachel for five hundred lirot as an advance for 'incidental expenses' and asked one of the messengers to take it to Dr Lustig for his counter-signature with the forms. Meanwhile I looked up the Professor's telephone number. When the messenger came back, which was almost immediately, I said to Rachel, "I've given you five hundred lirot for clothes and food and transportation." I handed her the cheque. "You can cash it at any post office if you show this authorisation (I gave it to her), but you ought to open an account at a bank, so that we can pay your salary into it. You're being paid from a Special Fund set up to assist people in need that are very special to this country. It is, of course, entirely legal, but I'd be obliged if you didn't tell everyone about it, or we'd get crowded out with the wrong applicants". (The thought of Rachel tattling with strangers about the source of her wages was, of course, ludicrous.) "I'll get you the Professor on the line and I think you ought to tell him you're moving in later today."

Rachel said doubtfully, "So much money?"

I dialled the number and a voice answered, "What?" I thought I might have disturbed him at a bad moment, but I learnt later that this was how Professor Strumpfeld always answered the telephone.

"I'm speaking from the Ministry of Welfare. We have found you a household help. Would you like to speak to her?" I heard a deep indrawn breath, and I hastily passed the receiver over to Rachel.

She said, "I am Rachel, the household help. I'll be moving in this evening. Does that suit you?" She spoke in German.

"Impossible. I'm too busy."

Rachel said: "Then would you please leave the key with a neighbour," and put the receiver back firmly in its cradle.

First round to Rachel.

"Had you heard of Professor Strumpfeld?" I asked her, with interest.

"Who hasn't? 'Das Wunderkind'."

Not all 'Wunderkinder' fulfil their early promise. Professor Strumpfeld had surpassed his. He was to philosophy what Einstein was to science and Picasso to art. A giant, he towered, perhaps above them all.

He had started his exceptional career toward the dizzying heights very early indeed. Left in the traditional cardboard box at the age of about two months, on the doorstep of the Jewish Orphanage in Frankfurt, the sharp sound of the bell brought a cleaning woman scurrying to the door. She saw a dim figure retreating in the murk of a Frankfurt rainy day. When she picked up the box, the infant therein gurgled at her in the most appealing way.

Instead of bringing the child to the Superintendent, she took it home with her, and then, on the following day, to her other employer, a fairly rich lady, very prominent in the Jewish community, to whom this precocious infant had the good sense to gurgle again, just as appealingly. Mrs Strumpfeld fell for him at once. She was a woman already in her late fifties, her own two children were grown up and far from the nest. Adoption of the child was difficult, because of her age. There was a queue of young, childless Jewish couples, some waiting already years to adopt an infant.

The Strumpfelds, however, were able to arrange 'foster care' status. It was understood that when a suitable permanent home became available, they would have to give the baby up.

This understanding was made even more perfect by their substantial annual contribution to the Orphanage. Somehow, a 'suitable home' never turned up, until the infant (they called him Karl) was already eight years old, and so adoptable, according to the Rules, by the somewhat elderly but immensely loving Strumpfelds.

Karl knew that he was adopted. It made no difference to him. He regarded the Strumpfelds as his parents in every way. He was a nice child; affectionate, lively, obedient and interested in almost everything (he drew the line only at German grammar). When he was thirteen, his parents were surprised to receive a letter from the Headmaster of the excellent school he attended, asking them to call on him. An appointment was arranged. The puzzled parents asked Karl if he had done anything wrong and made it quite clear they were willing to forgive. Karl couldn't think of a thing.

"No young lady in trouble?" asked Dr Strumpfeld (he was a Doctor of Law), man-to-man.

Karl assured him there was not and confessed himself equally astonished at the summons.

The interview did not begin auspiciously. After the usual greetings, the Headmaster said, poker-faced: "I want you to take your son Karl out of my school."

"What has he done?"

"Everything."

Mrs Strumpfeld bridled. "Nobody is all bad. Besides, I don't believe it. Karl is a sweet boy. Kindly explain."

The Headmaster said: "Karl entered our School when he was six years old. We put him, naturally, in the First Grade. His teacher discovered that not only could he read and write - he told her he taught himself when he was "nearly four" - but to her considerable embarrassment, he supplemented her lessons in every subject. For example, when she told the children, "the sun and the moon were very far away" he put up his hand, and, when questioned, gave the exact distances and a short discourse on how they were measured. Afterwards, he came over to the teacher's desk and offered in the most kindly manner to lend her a book. After several months of this demoralisation, she asked me to move him up to the second grade.

"Two months later, he was top of his class and his teacher told me she hadn't anything to teach him. He has now been seven years at our school. During this time, he has moved from grade 1 to grade 12, where he learns with, or, more accurately, teaches, 17 year olds.

Three months ago, at the desperate combined request of the eight specialists who prepare the 12th grade for university, we entered him for the University Entrance examinations for several of the top German universities. No one would have him. They all declared he must have cheated to obtain such high scores.

"We asked the University of Heidelberg to send down someone from the Philosophy Department - that's what he's most interested in - to examine him personally. They were a bit intrigued, and the Head of the Department came himself. He gave him a written and an oral examination.

"On the written examination he got ninety-eight out of a possible score of one hundred. I queried the Professor on what he lost the two points and he said bitterly "on his handwriting". As regards the oral, when I asked how Karl had done, the Professor replied even more bitterly, "There goes my Chair in ten years."

"So, please, take him away. Heidelberg will be glad to have him; for no fees, if that's a consideration. It's either he goes, or half my staff!"

The Strumpfelds were elated, proud, and frightened. They arranged for an elderly cousin to keep house for him and look after him in Heidelberg. When he entered the University, he was fourteen. By seventeen, he had his first degree in philosophy, and by nineteen, his doctorate and a research and teaching post. He would easily have beaten his Professor's prediction regarding a Chair by a couple of years if circumstances had not intervened, for, a year later, he published the first volume of his eight volume Treatise "The Nature of Truth, Belief and Reality". His earlier book, a critical study of Nietzsche, had already caused a stir in academic circles. This one, which was to philosophy what the Unified Field Theory was to Physics, and more, made him a household name. Before this, however, chronology began to play a part in his life.

Karl Strumpfeld had been born in 1915, on, according to an arbitrary decision of his new parents, the 1st day in May. This made him, at twenty-one, already a much acclaimed 'Wunderkind' and in steady succession towards his professorship at Heidelberg. The events of 1936, which saw Hitler's steady progress, changed his direction. He had no problem. The Strumpfelds were already planning to leave for Switzerland. (In the event, Dr Strumpfeld died suddenly and the widow stayed in Frankfurt, foolishly, to her doom.) But young Karl was not aware of this, and thus felt no obligations to stay in Germany. He made it known delicately through professional circles that he would welcome a change and the academic world beat a path to his door.

Out of a plethora of offers, he chose the gentle aura and liberal traditions of Cambridge, England, where he became a Fellow.

It was there, during 1936-1942, that he wrote the other seven volumes of his treatise. The University created a special Chair for him (History of Philosophy) with the aid of a rich donor who was stricken by the honour and astounded at his luck. He had been in competition not only with other men of wealth, but half a dozen British and International Companies who felt their faces needed a lift.

The British Government not only fell over its feet to grant this extraordinary refugee citizenship, but threw in an OBE, and a knighthood was in sight, when Professor Strumpfeld disappeared.

His behaviour had always been slightly eccentric. In 1939, he had turned up at a Recruiting Centre in Cambridge and asked to join the Army.

Recognising him (who in Cambridge did not? The flowing cape, the ever-smoking pipe), the officer in charge had a word with London, then told him the Intelligence people would be in touch, something in Whitehall or at one of these country houses.

Karl Strumpfeld said that was not what he had in mind. What he wanted to do was to be an infantry man in a fighting regiment. Since they could not argue him out of it, they turned him down on grounds of health. He promptly got himself a part-time voluntary job as a stretcher bearer at a military hospital near Cambridge.

It was said that when once he brought in an unconscious wounded soldier, who, as it happened, had been a student of his, the wounded man revived in transit, opened his eyes, saw Dr Strumpfeld and said weakly, "I must be dead and gone to hell," and promptly fainted again. He had not been a good student, and Professor Strumpfeld had never been a patient man. Stupidity, especially, made him very nasty indeed.

Professor Strumpfeld, having disappeared abruptly and without explanation from the Cambridge scene in 1942 when the war was still going rather badly for the Allies, turned up mysteriously a few weeks later in Palestine. How he got there, no-one knows. He immediately volunteered for the Jewish Brigade, and since the Recruiting Officer was a man of low education and impressive ignorance, he was accepted, and saw service in Italy, where he fought savagely, indeed as an infantry man, and was promoted to the rank of sergeant.

At the conclusion of the war he got himself transferred to a Supply Unit near Brindisi, a small depot consisting of about fifty men who looked after the needs of the British army personnel still remaining in Italy while the mopping up was being done and the Peace was being hammered out. At this time he spoke fluently English, German, Italian, and quite a lot of Hebrew which he had learnt from his mates. He spoke all these languages with accents indistinguishable from those of a cultured native. He also taught himself, and learned well, the ancient art of forgery. He could look at a signature, and reproduce it immediately to perfection.

The Head of the Supply Depot was a major whose main interests were drink and women, both in excellent supply. He was happy to leave command of the activities of the Unit to this new and impressively capable sergeant.

The Supply Command back home were somewhat puzzled by extraordinary increases in the needs of this obscure Unit, but bowed to the major's signature on demands for fifty personnel-carrying trucks, thousands of blankets, huge amounts of petrol, medicines, tinned foods and even, once, a few hundred packets of sanitary pads.

The military mind is not an enquiring one. The orders were checked, transcribed and sent. Nevertheless, there was a certain amount of comment when an order came through for six hundred sets of woollen winter underwear, size twelve.

"Christ, what the bloody hell are the Eyties doing to our lads out there?" asked the Head Storekeeper, "Shrinking them? They're turning them into fucking dwarfs, by God. Someone ought to look into this." But no-one did. Then, at any rate.

A later requisition sheet for one thousand pairs of ladies and children's knickers, assorted sizes, did cause the Stock-keeper to request an interview with the GOC (Supplies). A careful letter was sent to the Major at Brindisi, suggesting an explanation was in order. An immediate reply came in Sergeant Strumpfeld's version of the Major's flowing hand. He explained politely that Italians had money but no goods. The Unit, in introducing a barter system for fresh produce for the British Army, believed it was saving British soldiers from scurvy and reducing expenses for His Majesty's Armed Forces. "Stout Chap!" said the GOC. He then did something he would later regret. He shuffled out from among the papers on his desk the one headed 'Promotions'. Against the stock-keeper's name (staff-sergeant to second lieutenant) he wrote: "Unadvisable. Poor judgement. Not officer material."

Meanwhile, Sergeant Strumpfeld, in close liaison with other ex-Brigade members who were master-minding the flow of refugees from Camp to Camp, always in the direction of the Mediterranean ports of Italy, sat night after night by the telephone, sending blankets and clothing here and trucks there, and stayed up into the hours of the morning forging the logs of the trucks and accounting for the petrol usage.

Without him, literally thousands of "illegals" might never have reached the shores of Palestine. It took quite a long time before the sanitary towels (metaphorically) stuck in someone's throat, and then to crown it, a convoy of unfortunates was captured wrapped in British Army blankets and travelling on British army lorries.

The wrath that fell on Sergeant Strumpfeld's head was enormous. Treason or treachery would have been better - but to make a laughing-stock of the Supply Brigade! However, he languished in a British military prison for only a few months before someone found out who he was. There were red faces in Whitehall and even the King was said to be embarrassed. The fellow was got out quick to Palestine since that was where he said he wanted to go, with a minimum of fuss and a dishonourable discharge marked "Top Secret".

In Palestine, Professor Strumpfeld promptly joined the Haganah, and fought in the War of Independence. In this army, he felt greatly at home, since, although there were none of his eminence, there was a fair scattering of philosophers, many of them also from Germany.

He fought in one of the bloody battles for Latrun, lost an eye, met his Commander, Moshe Dayan, who greeted him: "Et tu Brute!" and then engaged him in a three hour conversation on the nature of the "I-thou" relationship according to Martin Buber.

At the conclusion of the war, a delegation from the Hebrew University of Jerusalem approached Professor Strumpfeld and offered him a Chair. He declined on the grounds that it would be too exhausting. As he put it, "you guys argue too much. Jesus Christ even couldn't teach you religion, so who am I to teach you philosophy?" They thought he was joking, but he was not.

When, timorously, the new and much smaller Tel Aviv University tried their luck, beating the traffic to the door of his modest flat in

North Tel Aviv, they were astonished when he said "yes". His only question had been, "How many students are there in the Faculty at present?" The Dean nervously explained it would be a new Faculty and there were not yet any students.

"Excellent," replied Professor Strumpfeld. "I'll take it." He then passed on to them a batch of telegrams from Harvard, Yale, Tokyo, Cambridge, the Sorbonne and so on, and asked if one of the secretaries could reply to them with his regrets. In the Autumn, the Professor conducted the first colloquium (he never lectured) to seven students, beginning with the statement "most philosophers have to work hard to obtain the necessary non-objectivity to ply their trade. Fate, however, has helped me by providing me with a constant one-eyed view." Here, he delicately touched his eyepatch. This talk was filmed (without permission) and made headlines even in the non-academic world.

Professor Strumpfeld's class grew with astonishing rapidity, students joining it from among the locals as well as from abroad. Visitors came too, from top level Academia. Tel Aviv University rapidly found itself the hub of the world, at any rate as far as Philosophy was concerned.

Karl Strumpfeld never got his knighthood from a ruffled King; but he did get honorary doctorates from every university of repute, and, even after his retirement, when he wrote what was assumed to be his final book, he was News.

There was no difficulty whatsoever in classifying him as very Special indeed.

Rachel rose to go. I said to her, nervously - I had been rehearsing it for hours - "Rachel, could we keep in touch? I mean, could we be friends? Nothing to do with a work relationship, just friends? I would so much like to get to know you." To my surprise, the smile Rachel gave me was nothing like the slightly grim half-smile, the smiles of irony and wry amusement I had seen before. Her face was irradiated and she looked at me warmly.

"Well, of course. I'd like to. I'd like to very much; I've never had a friend." Then she touched my hand and walked away with her light step, without saying when we could meet and without taking my home telephone number that I had prepared on a slip of paper, just in case. I didn't know if I'd ever see her again.

I got through my remaining clients with great rapidity. I was asking "Name, please," as they came in at the door. I got my usual fifty per cent score, that is, I could help half of them, the remainder either didn't really need help, or did, but there was no way I could give it. Social work is like teaching: it's not the time you spend that exhausts you, but the amount of effort and feeling you have to put into it. I was pretty tired by midday, and I thought I would take a break so I bought a sandwich at the cafe down the street, and went to eat it in the park.

5   ISRAEL, 1978

I sat down on a bench and I thought about my life, and why it was as it was, and what Rachel had to do with it. This last was far from clear. Everything else had been gone over many times before. My own probings and those of a very skilled Jungian psychoanalyst - it all added up to the same picture.

The people who had played significant roles in forming me, in bringing me to where I was, were my grandmother, my mother, and to a lesser degree, cousin Evelyn. All women. My father, except in the genetic sense, had hardly counted. My brother had counted for a great deal, but not as a person. He was 'sex'.

I only got to know my grandmother well when she came to live with us, when I was fourteen. She died, in a nursing home, when I was about sixteen. But long before we had this direct relationship, she played a huge role in my life, because she dominated my mother, and my mother dominated me.

Although she was my grandmother, she was known to everyone (except my mother) as Tanta, which I think means 'aunt' in some mid-European language, like 'tante' in French. Likewise, my grandfather was known to us all as "Uncle".

Uncle was born in London, to an immigrant family from Kiev. They lived in Whitechapel, in London's East End, along with all the other poverty-stricken Jewish immigrants. Uncle put himself through High School by stuffing sausages for the butcher and wrapping fish. He never delivered newspapers, because no-one where he lived could afford a newspaper. Nor could many read anything but Yiddish. Yet, strangely enough, he became a publisher, and not in English, which he knew because he attended school, but in Yiddish, which he didn't know well at all.

Of course there was no money in it. He wasn't the kind of publisher that took talented ladies to expensive lunches to talk about royalties. He published Yiddish writers because there were so many of them flowering in this ghetto, and they were so good! Novelists, essayists, and, of course, poets.

Sales were not good. The Yiddish speaking community was avid for reading material but few were in a position to buy books except as a rare treat. So books 'circulated'. The writer didn't make a living, but, if barely, Uncle could. Especially as he passed on to his printer odd jobs, wedding invitations and the like, for which he took a small commission. They added up. No-one expected to live on literature, it was a luxury, and his mother scolded Uncle and nagged him to take up a proper job, like tailoring or selling shirts.

But Uncle paid no heed. He never became even mildly prosperous, he never managed to join the flood of Jews out of the East End and into Stanford Hill, and then even into Golder's Green. But he ate three times a day, and when he was part of a welcoming committee to new immigrants from Russia, from "der Heim", bewildered people under the impression that they were arriving at what they had paid for, "Amerike, New York," he was able to offer a wedding ring and two rooms and kitchen to a charming young girl from Moldavia, who metamorphosed through the years into our "Tanta".

Tanta, of course, spoke only Yiddish. She also knew enough Hebrew - rare for a girl - to get a job teaching First Grade in Hebrew School. But it didn't last long. The interest in Hebrew was not high in Whitechapel. She would have done better with horse-riding or other such would-be upper class pursuits.

Tanta became a housewife, and, subsequently, also a mother. She was apparently rotten at both. She never ever learned English well, and her shopping was a disaster. For many years, it was conducted mostly in mime, and when she did learn the words, she mispronounced them horribly. "You got a lettel feesh?" with difficulty obtained her a haddock.

Like all good housewives, she scrubbed her floors every week, and then laid down newspapers on them, like setting up a delightful jumping game, so as to retain their pristine Lifebuoy soap purity at least over Sabbath. But here Tanta's resemblance to other lower-class housewives ended. While spreading her (Yiddish) newspapers, she would get interested in them, sit down on the floor and begin to read.

One o'clock would come, and with it Uncle, hungry for his lunch, but Tanta would be absorbed in politics, literature, poetry and just plain news. She was a true intellectual. Everything interested her - that is, everything that was abstract and impersonal. She didn't hold daily life in the practical sense in much esteem.

She wrote poetry, too, and got it published, not in Uncle's newspaper, but in well-known ones in New York. Uncle, although proud of her in a way, would rather have had a well-run comfortable home. Tanta regarded Uncle much as a nervous worker regards punching in the time clock every morning. Her days were constant battles to have things right for Uncle - meals on the table (in time), pyjamas washed and laid out, always a clean shirt - these were not heavy demands for another type of woman. For Tanta they were sheer hell. Was she afraid of Uncle? They had no intimacy, never talked, almost never went out together. Uncle was not frightening in any real sense - but he was very detached and very big. He was also a man of habit.

There was Uncle's chair, and Uncle's radio and Uncle's jar of sweets, all strictly off limits to Tanta and their child. Things ran against Tanta, too. Clocks in the house only worked if you laid them on their side or upside down. Doors jammed, or wouldn't shut at all. Tanta always felt that her house was against her.

To my mother, her only child, born quite a number of years after her marriage, Tanta reacted with dutiful amazement. She was not a natural infant lover and my mother, as a baby, as a child, as a young girl, quickly exhausted her interest. She didn't understand about toys and building blocks and skipping ropes; and dressing like the other kids, giggling over boys.

When this person she lived with showed no interest in Marxism, or (early) feminism, or the trade balance, she decided her daughter was stupid. She treated her fairly and kindly, and restrained her conversations with her to telling her what to do. She never listened to her at all. Later, she paid dearly for this.

My poor mother, her protests ignored, suffered also from Tanta's slight eccentricities. For example, she dearly loved a bargain. What she liked best was materials (her father had been a cloth merchant, among other things). At sale times, she hit the better shops, making a direct line to the huge baskets marked 'remnants'. When it came to remnants, Tanta knew no restraint; no sense of reality held her back. If a dress required two and a half yards of material, Tanta regarded a one yard nine inch piece simply as a challenge for a dressmaker's skills. The nineteen inch length of rich brocade (just inadequate for a blouse), that small piece of embroidered muslin, fragments of cloche, the single yard of fine serge, the tweed, the real silk and damask, the rich linen - she bought them all at a fraction of the usual cost. They were all intended for my mother. Tanta didn't care about her own dress.

She found a patient dressmaker. Together, they contrived. There were false hems, clever cutting, and lace or other additions in unspeakable combinations. For years my mother wore only short tight skirts, and sleeveless blouses with false backs that could be worn only with a jacket, or with inserts of strange contrasting materials; and straight, skimpy dresses with low necks, stretched across her developing bosom. While her chums bounded about in cheap, ready made, pretty cottons, with wide flared skirts and puffy sleeves or extravagant blouses in cheap artificial silk over generous pleated skirts.

It all came from C & A, or suchlike mass-production stores, and cost hardly more than my mother's masterpieces that never wore out, that wore and wore; as she outgrew them, she seemed to pour out of them at every aperture.

My mother never forgave or forgot. The Tanta-produced agonies, the snickers in the school cloakrooms, were etched into her. It had not been a happy childhood. The day she left home, she swore she would never ever buy any garment except ready made ones again in her life, and she never did. She also hated 'bargains' - whatever she was buying, she would walk into the shop and announce simply, "I'm willing to pay for the best!" It was a costly way to live.

Tanta, convinced that her child was not all that bright, nevertheless sent her to university, to learn to be a teacher. She did not think highly of teachers. Despite her deep conviction that whatever Tanta wanted for her must be wrong, my mother actually liked teaching. For once, she was at the helm. Tanta, of course, would have preferred to have produced a Sappho, an Emily Dickinson, an Elizabeth Barratt Browning or an ill-fated Rosa Luxembourg. She did the best she could. There was no love in Tanta's heart for her only child, but there was no hate either. Dispassionately, objectively, she wished her well.

Starting, to my knowledge, with Tanta, the emotional heritage in my family seemed to go down from generation to generation via the female line, and in a skewed fashion. Tanta had a niece, whom she loved, Sally; a woman a bit like her from a branch of the family that still lived in the Ukraine. Sally wrote poetry too - but in English, she was a whizz at languages. A year off the boat and she wrote, read and spoke English like a native. She took a lively interest in world affairs. Since she was more worldly, softer, more in tune with her surroundings, she was also able to be close to my mother, becoming in many ways the mother she never had. Sally had two daughters, my cousins Margaret and Evelyn. Margaret was the adored one, Evelyn was tolerated. Yet it was cousin Evelyn who most resembled Sally and who, in our strange dynasty, became my mother's confidant and friend and eventually forged a bond with me.

From my earliest childhood, she was my authority on what was right and beautiful and good. The twist here, however, was different. I did not hate my mother as she hated hers. I wasn't too sure about her judgement in worldly terms, like what kind of picture to hang on my bedroom wall, but I loved her. My mother and I always talked about such matters, then we would decide, jointly and harmoniously, that cousin Evelyn should be consulted. The dynasty persisted.

Where were the men in all this? Strictly adjuncts, out at the edge of the field.

Except, of course, for my brother Uri.

My mother found my father-to-be in Palestine, in 1938, when on a visit to one of her distant cousins.

She fell in love with him instantly. He was a gentle, amiable man. It took him a bit longer to make up his mind, and before he did, he joined the British Army, and went missing in Italy in 1942, but then got found again, was sent to Britain, where they married at once. My mother followed him when he was transferred back to the Middle East. She took an apartment in Jerusalem, and she sweated it out while he fought in the desert battles against Rommel. As a result of one of his rare leaves, my brother Uri was born in 1944. I followed after the War, in 1945, after he returned to live in Jerusalem. My father got a job as a rather junior administrator in the Jewish Agency, but in his out-of-office hours he helped run an illegal radio station which the British never found. With its help, the Jews were organising for the War of Independence. My mother, being a teacher, taught.

Uncle and Tanta continued their placid existence - to the extent that existence in wartime England, and London in particular, could be called placid. There was bombing. There was not, of course, much to eat. Uncle's business ran slowly down and he worked part-time in a factory while still doggedly publishing what there was of Yiddish belles lettres, novellas, stories and poetry.

Tanta still wrote her poems which she sent to a New York Yiddish newspaper where they got published and she still kept her 'open house' on Friday nights for those of the intellectuals who could manage to get there, despite the blackouts and the bombings. (Their street was never struck).

Shortly after the War ended, Uncle's printer packed it up. The new generation of Jews, even those still caught in what was left of the East End of London after the fire bombs, didn't know Yiddish, or certainly not as a language to be read. It was for talking to the parents, for a curse, or a joke. To make a relationship. To make a business customer feel a friend.

Books were Moby Dick and Sherlock Holmes and you got them from the public library. Who needed to 'own' a book?

He offered his printing press to Uncle at a suitable loss, and got from his Union what was essentially a retirement job, collecting dues. He loved it. He liked to walk. He didn't mind rain or sun. He liked to chat, about Socialism and little known heroes of the British Left, Keir Hardie, Harry Pollitt and the like.

"Morning, Mrs Jones. Union dues. Two months, I see, that will be two shillings."

"Morning. Won't you come in? Sorry about last month, it was the wedding, you see. Our oldest. Took every penny we had. Married a nice young man, in tailoring, a real go-getter. He'll end up with his own shop, mark my words. Was just making a cup. Feel like one? Very cold weather for the time of year."

Of course he felt like one; strong, sweetened with condensed milk and served with a Marie biscuit. And he could take his time. No-one pushed.

Uncle crated up the printing press and sent it to Jerusalem. Then he sold his house. He packed up his furniture and personal belongings, including Tanta, and they travelled by ship to the Middle East, wholly unknown territory, to an apartment within walking distance of their only child, which she had reluctantly rented for them. They arrived in the middle of a war, only a few weeks after the proclamation of the State of Israel. Uncle ignored the war and set up his printing press, of necessity, single-handed. There were no young men around.

Was it parental love, or just following a path towards a better living? Certainly, in England, Yiddish was dead or dying. In Israel, although the handwriting was on the wall, there was still a living to be made from Yiddish, and it would outlast Uncle, certainly, before Hebrew took over as it did.

Tanta took to Israel like a duck to water. There was a plethora of writers, artists, musicians, waiting to be gathered in. But this was 1948 already, and something was happening to Tanta.

As long as my mother remembered, there had been the letters. Grey envelopes of poor quality, coarse paper (recycled or just poorly made?) from Moldavia, from Poland, from the Ukraine.

Tanta was one of a large family, three brothers, four sisters. They had all married, and in due course produced nephews and nieces.

Tanta wrote to, and was written to, by them all. Every week at least, there was a letter, with the strange, foreign handwriting and the strange, foreign stamps. Sometimes, inside, a chalk or crayon drawing from one or another of the children, making a statement of their existence to the unknown aunt in a far away land.

Tanta always pinned up the drawing in her kitchen, till the next one came to replace it. She never pinned up the drawings her child brought home from school. Tanta read each letter many times over, opening them at once, stopping whatever she was doing. Was this then the secret of the cold intellectual Tanta we knew - she could love, she was loving, but it was all for the family 'back there'; nothing for the strangers amidst whom she lived her strange life in this strange place? Emotionally, had Tanta never left the wooden house, the family, the village, "der alte Heim"?

In 1940, Tanta had stopped getting letters. She understood. There was a war on. One only had to wait. Tanta waited. At the end of the war there were still no letters. She began her long search.

She, who knew so little in practice of the world around her, learned quickly. She applied to all the refugee organisations, to the Occupation Authorities (including the Russians, to whom she wrote in Russian), to the Jewish Agency, (and later, the Israeli Government), to the United Nations, the list was long. Tanta's spidery foreign writing, and copies of photographs, lists of names (she couldn't remember all the nieces and nephews, and how old would they be now?), addresses of small towns that no longer existed on the face of the earth. She advertised in newspapers. She sent letters to the mayors or the officers-in-charge of these small towns. Tanta searched for three years for her family; others were lucky, but Tanta was not. She could not find a single survivor, all had gone, disappeared into the inferno, who knows, the gas chamber in

Auschwitz, the pit in Babi Yar? Not even a cousin or a friend. Not even the neighbour across the street.

In 1948, less than a year after her arrival in Jerusalem, Tanta gave up. She put her photographs back in their albums. She stopped writing poetry too, at that time, and her salons, her 'Friday evenings' began to wither away, like a plant whose roots have been destroyed.

Tanta became an old lady, rather like any other. She did not talk much. Her eyes did not gleam with enthusiasm about politics or art or anything at all.

In the late nineteen-fifties, Uncle died, of a stroke. Cholent, that mixture of beef, beans, potatoes, slowly cooked in the oven (not an ideal dish for an exceptionally hot summer's day in Jerusalem) was his undoing. Uncle collapsed, and died on his way to the hospital. For a time, Tanta uncomplainingly failed to manage on her own. Since there were no demands on her, she simply did nothing.

My mother couldn't cope with looking after Tanta's apartment, as well as her own, with the cleaning and the shopping and the cooking. So, without enthusiasm on either side, Tanta came to live with us.

My mother ordered her around a lot. Tanta took it, meekly, submissively. I suppose she couldn't help it, but I never forgave my mother for taking her long-awaited revenge.

When Tanta came to live with us, I had troubles of my own. I had had them for a long time, perhaps ever since I could remember, but I was fourteen years old now and they were coming to a head.

It was my brother Uri. I can't say, in the delicate euphemism, that he actually "interfered with me", but at times it was pretty near. This sexual interest (which, of course, I had not at first recognised as such) began with too many kisses, too much fondling, too much taking me on his knee; probably when I was about three. Later he began to sneak into my bed at night, he would kiss me and touch my breasts, and then there was a hand between my legs. As long as I remember I always felt it was 'wrong'. I didn't like him. When I got older, I began to threaten him and to lock my bedroom door. He was afraid and desisted, but still, occasionally, there would be that soft knock on the door, that soft voice I now hated and feared: "Gerda, let me in. I promise..."

When Tanta came, she shared my bedroom, and that put an end to that. Or was my mother more aware than I thought? She did not like Uri. Maybe that was the trouble.

Anyway, I was grateful to Tanta, and I liked her. She was no bother at all. I could not understand, at that time, why she incensed my mother so. She couldn't lift a broom and dust pan without my mother shrieking: "What do you think you're doing? You know you can't do anything right." My mother's revenge was only a reflection of the depth of her pain.

Did Tanta feel my sympathy? She began to talk to me. She had left Moldavia when she was twenty. She had spent fifty years in the West. Yet all she spoke about was the 'old country', as if her later life, Uncle, the poets and politics, her child, were of no significance at all.

She told me about Sheindele and Hannele, and Golda and Sarale, and Moishe and Shlomo, sisters and brothers, cousins, and friends. She told me about her father and mother and their cow and their three goats and the sheep. About bathing in the river, candles on Sabbath, and white bread in the basket lined with a cloth of white lace. She would pluck my sleeve and lead me to a corner, and it came pouring out, the love, the sorrow, and, of course, the guilt that she was alive. The intellectual Tanta sometimes revived a bit and she would talk in the old way to my parents or their guests, slowly though, and with little of the old enthusiasm.

But me, she took back to her family, her home, to me she released the burden of her love.

Tanta's stay with us wasn't very long. After only a year, my mother couldn't stand it any more. Besides, Tanta was getting forgetful. Sometimes she forgot to dress. This embarrassed my mother, but it didn't embarrass me. There was no way I could be unaffected by her confidences; I loved her.

My mother found her "a place". An old friend, widowed young and with grown up children, took in old people and looked after them - to some extent. She was cool, detached, capable and not unkind. She was entirely devoid of genuine human understanding. My mother put Tanta there, into a gloomy bedroom, with over-powering, heavy Germanic furniture, solid mahogany built to last. Perhaps Tanta minded it less than I did. It spoke to me of death.

Tanta's banishment so upset me that the night after she left, when Uri came to my door, I unlocked it, let him in, and hit him with all my strength. I had taken a kitchen knife, and I showed him it.

"If you bother me again, if you ever so much as come near me, I'll stick this in your guts."

"I don't know what you're talking about." Sulky.

"You know. Get out!"

He got out. He never tried to touch me again. Quite soon after this episode, he announced he wanted to go to a Navy boarding school. Both my parents were pleased, for different reasons. I almost never saw him again. I still almost never see him. But he had left his mark alright. I wanted never to be touched by men. Even talking to a boy aroused the old fear. I wished fervently for a world of women.

Maybe I will never ever get over this, entirely. It wasn't till I was thirty that I was able to go to bed with a man at all, and even then, although it was alright, it wasn't really a success. Since then, essentially, brief affairs, putting up with the sexual side for the sake of the rest of it all.

I used to go with my mother to visit Tanta, once or twice a week. She had taken to her bed, although I didn't think there was any physical reason for this. My mother would chatter brightly and tell her all the news. Tanta rarely responded.

"Senile," my mother would say to me afterwards, with satisfaction. "I got her settled just in time."

Mother's friend would come in with a tray. Tea for all of us. There would be unappetising slices of nourishing black bread and margarine and jam, a plastic unbreakable mug for Tanta, a ridiculous yellow child's mug with a picture of Mickey Mouse, tea-cups for us, old German china. My mother would spoon Tanta her tea and put a slice of bread into her hand. Sometimes she nibbled on it, obediently, sometimes she didn't. Then my mother would go downstairs to chat with her friend. Tanta would sit up, and take my hand. Her eyes would brighten, her speech would become more coherent, her voice stronger.

"You look so much like Sheindele," she would begin, and then on and on. She spoke about a quiet village, a world of Jews, all gone, vanished without any traces, the burned synagogue, the dug up desecrated graves, the pits with no graves, the field with its burden of bones. Tanta saw nothing of this. It was a golden day in summer, mother was milking the cow, father had gone off to "do a business deal" (perhaps involving one more goat), Tanta and Sheindele were in the barn, talking about their older sister's forthcoming wedding and what they would wear.

"I had one white dress," said Tanta, tossing her strong black hair in the golden sun, "and I said to Sheindele, 'you have it. I will make myself something else to wear'. We didn't even have knickers," said Tanta happily. "We were too poor."

Mother would come to fetch me when it was time to go home. "Kiss Tanta goodbye," she would say, after delivering her own dutiful peck. "See you next week." I'd kiss Tanta, she would look at me and see my love for her in my eyes, love and pity, I couldn't distinguish one from the other.

"Sheindele," Tanta would say tenderly, and kiss me back. "Like Sheindele." Almost inaudibly.

"You see, she's rambling. Doesn't know who you are," said my mother triumphantly.

She knew.

I was the one who closed her eyes. I was the one who wept at her funeral, I was the one who received this heritage, the hot sun, the fields, the barn, and the other sisters and brothers, the cousins, the child Sheindele, lime pits with the burnt flesh and the splintered bones. Tanta gave me all this, injected into my blood, as surely as if by a hypodermic syringe.

I got over Uri, more or less, like you get over a long serious illness - a bit impaired, but ready to go on. I never got over Tanta. You never get over love. Everything she left me stays with me.

I got up and went home. I took a shower and went to bed. Sometimes I can sleep it off.

When I woke up the room was dark but I had left my bed lamp on. The light was shining in my face. Suddenly, I had a great golden flash of understanding. Tanta was Rachel, Rachel was Tanta. They were one and the same.

Later, I realised that, like all such phenomena, it did not stand up to any smattering of logic. They were both strong women. There, all similarity ended. Yet it was so.

6. ISRAEL, 1978, GERMANY, 1942

I was sitting opposite her, at the Rowal. I had waited two weeks and, at last, she had phoned me. Counting the days.

"Gerda, would you like to have a cup of coffee with me?" Same Arabic-sounding German. Would I!

"Sure, when and where?"

Faintly surprised. "Now, of course. You tell me where. I don't know any places."

"Rowal Café, Dizengoff Street. It's quite famous, anyone will direct you. See you in about half an hour?"

"Dizengoff Street. Near the Centre? Where the coloured ice-water cake is?" Ice water cake, wedding cake, merry-go-round, Agam's expensive blunder; waterfalls, gaudy coloured lights and music - it is rumoured that it costs the city twenty thousand ill-spent dollars a year to run it. At least it's always a recognisable landmark.

"Quite near. See you."

And she was there, sitting with a book in front of her. I can't say I hardly recognised her - I could spot Rachel among a million people - but her appearance had certainly changed. She had her hair piled up, instead of straggling around her face, and she wore jeans and a blouse and sandals on her bare feet; in other words, typical Israeli uniform, same for all ages, all sizes, all types.

These clothes revealed an abundance of full, firm curves - in her Arab dress she had been the usual shapeless lump. She didn't look young, of course, but matronly in an appealing way, what used to be called approvingly in Victorian novels "a fine figure of a woman" till times changed and Twiggy took over. Her grey eyes were, as always, beautiful. They told me she knew everything. She knew everything I needed to know. I said, "Hello, what's your book?"

She closed it. "Wittgenstein's 'Reflections'." It was in German, of course.

"You've taken to heavy reading. The Professor's influence, I suppose?"

"In a way. It makes his Hebrew lessons easier to understand." I wondered if the ability to reflect in Hebrew on the meaning of language would help her much in buying a tee-shirt at the Shuk or a bus ticket to Haifa, but held my peace.

She offered an explanation. "It makes the lessons interesting for him."

"And for you?"

"Oh yes. For me too."

The same Rachel after all. Brief, withdrawn. I asked the waiter for coffee. Then I threw my line out swiftly, without bothering about bait or tackle.

"What happened to you, there?" I asked.

"What do you mean?"

I was afraid she wouldn't answer me. Then: "After you were at the Military Camp with the SS Colonel. When you thought it would last forever. It didn't though, did it?"

"No. I didn't understand. None of us understood. We thought they wanted sex. We thought we could hold on to life by offering them always new, exciting sex. They didn't, though. What they wanted was love. Like all men, even from whores they wanted love."

"So he got tired of you, the Colonel?"

"Not yet. He would have. But as it happened, he blotted his copybook," (the German idiom was different). "He quarrelled with somebody's nephew and hurt him badly in a duel. They fought duels. They thought a lot about their 'honour'. So he got sent to a fighting unit. Probably in Russia. He bought a fur coat."

"And you?"

"He put me on a train to Munich with a letter to his brother. I managed to open and read it on the way. It said, 'The bearer of this is a little Jewish whore. I am going to the Front and may not come back. In any event will you look after her for me? If she doesn't please you, will you send her to our country place till all this is over? Kiss Mutti for me. Your loving brother'."

"Did you find him? Did you give him the letter?"

"Oh yes."

"What did he say? What did he do?"

"He didn't say anything. He pointed to the door. Then we got in his car and he drove me to a Police Station. He marched me inside and said to the sergeant at the desk: 'This is a Jewish whore. Do with her what you think fit.' There were two other policemen in the room."

"What did they decide?" It was like pulling teeth.

"Well, first they decided to have some fun. So they did. Then they had to think how to get rid of me, and one of them had a bright idea. "There's a transport going out today. Let's take her down to the railway station." They took me there. Hundreds of Jews in a long line. SS men with dogs and whips and guns. Important businessmen shitting in their pants with good reason. I was pushed into the line. A woman said to me, 'But you have no suitcase. Didn't you bring any working clothes?'

"I don't need any working clothes." I thought I would be sent back to the military camp."

"And were you?"

"No, I was sent to another kind of Camp. Mauthausen." Firmly: "Would you like another cup of coffee? It's very pleasant here."

It was. Early dark. Mediterranean faces. European faces. Girls mostly with little or no make-up, many youngsters, many in Army uniform, but everyone bright, animated, strolling, so much to tell each other, a new film, a video clip, a new posting, another stripe. A few oldsters, cautious steps in the waning sun. Business people (not shitting in their pants), working people, going shopping or going home. Minuscule Big City Tel Aviv throbs like a metropolis. Friendly ships that pass in the night. We watched, for a while. Rowal is, of course, mainly a pavement café. Rachel was monosyllabic again, a question and answer session; "yes," she liked the Professor; "no," the work wasn't too hard; "yes," she had enough money; "no," she hadn't yet found a flat.

Then there was silence, which was better, and eventually became very good. When we parted, she said it had been lovely and she would call me again.

I was happy. I was in her life.

Nevertheless, it was several weeks before I saw her again, and I didn't even notice it, much. Something momentous happened to me. Avi.

It's my uncaring habit to buy lots of food at the local supermarket, and eat well for several days till things start to go brown and dry and tasteless and eventually get thrown out. A wasteful way of living. Some sort of statement, I suppose. When the refrigerator is really empty, the last withered leaf of lettuce gone, the tomatoes mouldy, the bread dusty grey or pale green - I never buy food that needs much cooking, at least, I didn't then - I go downstairs with my shopping bags - no need to take the car, the supermarket is just one block away - I stock up again. A dreary, repetitive process, necessary, like cleaning your teeth. I wasn't into food, like I wasn't into anything much, then.

I didn't need a list. It was always the same: cereal, eggs, bread, sausage, soft drinks, coffee, butter, milk, fruit and vegetables. And of course, chocolate. I'm a chocolate addict. They say it's the caffeine, but I know better. I needed something sweet.

I picked up everything I wanted, pushed my trolley to a cash desk, paid, loaded everything into my shopping bags - the string of one of them was broken, so I had to carry it under one arm. It had been broken for weeks; of course I'd never mend it, one day I'd just toss it out and buy another.

Head down, wary eyes on a packet of butter that was trying to pop out, I ran into a head-on collision with a man. Avi.

The butter popped out, of course, plus a lot of other things. The eggs, naturally. Then the whole bag hit the floor, glass crunched, and a mess of bread and lemonade and eggs started to grow into a pool around me.

"Omigod!" said Avi. "I'm terribly, terribly sorry." Young man. No, youngish man. Slight. Dark. Moroccan origin maybe? Nice face. Nice eyes. Neatly dressed, but not over-dressed, blue shirt, grey trousers..

He looked at me. Then we both looked at the growing pool at our feet. A cucumber slowly joined it and then two apples. It looked obscene. Spontaneously, we stared at each other and then burst out into laughter.

"Come on. We'll restock you. Then, for safety, I'll escort you home."

"I wouldn't dream of it. It was my fault. I wasn't looking where I was going."

He didn't argue. He just took my arm and led me back into the aisles. He filled the cart with huge quantities of foods I would never think of buying, like mushrooms and asparagus and even smoked salmon; luxury foods. When I tried to pay, he said nothing, just took my purse and shoved it back firmly in my pocket. He paid with a credit card. Respectable.

"Where do you live?"

I told him.

"So we won't need a car. I'll just walk you up. Fourth floor, no lift, I bet?" He was right, of course.

He insisted on putting the food in the refrigerator.

"I'm not that clumsy," I said, coldly. "I can manage to get it in by myself."

"I'm taking no chances. You've already cost me more than dinner out and a movie and I've only just met you."

I offered him a cup of coffee, and he said 'yes' and then we sat and chatted about the things Israelis talk about, movies and concerts and whom you like in them and pubs, where you worked and the state of the country. After that, he said, "Can I phone you?"

"Of course. After all, we've broken bread together." I gave him my phone number, miserably. If they make a date on the spot, it might turn out to be something or it mightn't, but it's a beginning at least. When they ask for your phone number, they rarely ever call. So I gave him it, regretfully. I liked him. Avi. I even liked his name, simple and direct, just as he was.

It was Dr Lustig who told me about the first encounter between Rachel and Professor Strumpfeld.

7. ISRAEL, 1978

Dr Lustig liked to visit the 'Special' people from time to time. They were usually interesting people. As was, to him, also Rachel.

Reconstructing: Rachel did her shopping and arrived at the Professor's house late, tired and hungry. She found a note pinned to the door.

> "Dear Ms(?),
>
> The key to the front door is with the neighbour on the left. Please lock it securely after entering. Your room is the second on the upper floor. Please make no noise. You may return the key to me and receive further instructions tomorrow (4th May) at 10 a.m. Please be prompt. I will be in my study (ground floor, 2nd left).
> Very sincerely,   Strumpfeld."

At the end, as an afterthought, the Professor had added, "I hope you sleep well." Rachel smiled.

She took her belongings up to her room, which was old German-style Bauhaus, but with a new and comfortable bed. Then she took the food packages and went down into the kitchen and unpacked them and placed them wherever she thought was sensible. There seemed to be very little food in the house - coffee, sugar, baked beans (a sentimental reminder of England?) and a tin of Bartlett pears (likewise), half a loaf of bread (rather old). In the refrigerator, a carton of milk, an orange, a plastic bag containing sliced sausage (rancid), another with ham, a plate with a piece of nondescript local cheese masquerading as cheddar.

With an economy of movement that matched her economy of speech, she whipped up two eggs together with a dollop of milk, and stirred in freshly chopped basil and rosemary leaves. She heated a pitta bread over an open gas flame, and rubbed it with olive oil, garlic and tomato, peasant food; made some strong black coffee and settled down to eat. The omelette was cooked in olive oil too, a good raw green oil with a tangy taste.

Professor Strumpfeld had been in remission for several weeks and had regained some appetite. A natural bachelor, he had been living on cold meats, sausage and ham, cheeses, anything that didn't have to be cooked. The fragrance of Rachel's omelette, permeating to his bedroom, unmanned him. His mouth watered. He fought a brief battle with himself, lost, and descended to the kitchen.

"Good evening. I suppose you're Rachel?"

"Yes."

A long pause. A hesitant voice. "I'm rather hungry, for a change. I suppose you couldn't make me an omelette like that one?"

"Certainly." Rachel stood up.

"No, no, finish your meal first. I'm not in any hurry." Rachel paused for a minute. Then she took her plate with the remaining food on it and placed it on the warming rack of the oven.

"It takes only a minute," she said. "Then we can eat together."

It really did take only a few minutes. Professor Strumpfeld had forgotten that food could taste so good. He regarded Rachel amicably. "That was superb." His plate was clean. Not even a pitta crumb.

"I'm pleased."

"Since you're obviously an expert, can I ask you to cook for me? I'm not a fussy man. Anything you feel you can do."

Rachel said: "I'll try."

The Professor regained, with an effort, the position from which he had started.

"I shall want," he said, "breakfast at nine, lunch at one and dinner at seven-thirty and I would be obliged if you would be prompt. I can't afford to waste time, I've got work to do before I die. You can do all the shopping and whatever housework you care to do. I told you I'm not fussy. Dust doesn't bother me. You never, repeat, never come into my study or my bedroom without my express permission. Otherwise, you do what you like, except make noise. Is that clear? Does that suit you? Any questions?"

"It suits me. How do you want to arrange housekeeping money?"

"I'll give you a cheque. When the money's gone, ask for more." He looked at Rachel closely, into her deep grey eyes. What he saw decided him. "Don't bother with accounts or receipts," he said gruffly. "I've no time for things like that."

"I could steal you blind."

"I don't think so. Somehow, I don't think so."

He got up. A thought suddenly occurred to him. It was an unusual kind of thought, for it concerned neither philosophy nor himself.

"Is there anything you want?"

"Yes."

He waited for her to continue, but, as usual, Rachel did not. He grinned, intrigued, and said magnanimously, "Name it." In the secret account he would keep from now on, he chalked up one for Rachel.

She hesitated. "Can I have a day off once a week? It doesn't matter which day. I could be back by about seven, in time to make dinner. I'd go after breakfast and I could leave you a cold lunch in the refrigerator or something for heating up in the oven."

"Certainly. That is perfectly reasonable. Anything else?"

"Yes. Would you teach me Hebrew?"

"Good God, woman! I'm not a Hebrew teacher."

"I know. But if you taught me I wouldn't need to leave the house to take lessons and I do have to learn. Say, just three hours a week?"

The Professor pondered this. He knew very well there might be a time that he would not want Rachel to leave the house. He did not wish to think about this, so he thought about giving Rachel Hebrew lessons. It would take time from his work. On the other hand, it might be rather refreshing. Although languages were tricky, he was convinced she would be a good pupil. He also, although he would not have admitted this even to himself, found her company both challenging and soothing; like a good chess game.

After a minute he made up his mind. "You can have Tuesdays off. Mondays, Wednesdays and Fridays I'll give you a Hebrew lesson for one hour starting at 4 p.m. prompt. Agreed?"

"Agreed."

"Anything else?"

A shake of the head.

"Then in that case I wish you a very good night."

As he was about to leave, Rachel suddenly said, "There is one thing."

"Yes?"

"I'm not really a good cook."

A rare smile. "You'll do," he said.

Some of how their relationship progressed I learnt in the months that followed from Dr Lustig. Professor Strumpfeld was not a confiding man, nor one who made friends easily, or even at all. Dr Lustig, however, became the nearest one could get to becoming his old crony.

They had very similar backgrounds: bourgeois families, German schools and Universities, the exile in England, the army, Israel. (Dr Lustig, of course, did not know anything about philosophy. His subject was medieval German history). They developed a mutual fondness and respect. Dr Lustig not only received the Professor's confidences, he had no shame in laboriously pumping information out of Rachel.

But of her own affairs, she spoke only to me.

The ménage at the Professor's was, from the start, a success. Beginning, each, with a measure of mutual liking, approval and suspicion, they settled into a routine. Rachel extended her range of cooking from Arab to French and Italian and even Chinese. She did this in a serious way, buying cookbooks and reading them through, marking the recipes she thought she could handle.

She and the Professor ate together, at his insistence, but otherwise he hardly saw her save at Hebrew lessons, when she presented herself promptly in his study at the agreed time. He had no idea how to teach a language, so he simply picked out from his shelves the first book in German that caught his eye and translated passages for her.

She copied it all down, at first in transliteration; later, after she had learnt the alphabet, in Hebrew letters. He corrected her spelling, got interested, explained to her something about word roots and grammar. She was extremely attentive and did a great deal of homework. The Professor was pleased with her progress. At meals, they began to talk in a mixture of German and Hebrew - when they talked. Some meals passed in silence. Neither minded.

She never asked him about his illness. But when he began to leave half his food on the plate, Rachel's cooking became sharper, spicier and more adventurous. He never asked her where she went on her Tuesdays.

I did, though.

On Sunday, Professor Strumpfeld was picked up by a friend, and taken to his home for dinner and a game of chess. Rachel was free, and we began, more or less regularly, to meet on those evenings over a bowl of goulash soup (going strong to this day) at Hamozeg.

I was getting bolder, but not yet bold enough to be able to ask her about Mauthausen and whatever came after. That would come later. Tuesdays, I thought, would be easy. Maybe a trip to a shopping mall, window shopping, lunch and a movie - what most women did on the precious day of freedom from work or household chores.

It proved not to be easy at all. Rachel at her most curt, most evasive.

Eventually, I dragged out of her that she went to Jerusalem.

"Why Jerusalem? Memories of the past?" After all, it was in Jerusalem she had met her young Arab husband, been courted and got married and set up house; hopefully, had been happy, at least for a time.

"In a way."

I was persistent. She would only tell me what she wanted, but it doesn't hurt to be a bit of a nudnik. This time it helped. We had finished our soup, and were waiting for coffee and one of Hamozeg's huge portions of strudel, which we would share. The waiter knew us already. He always brought two plates and forks.

"Why does it interest you? I go to visit my daughter."

"Everything about you interests me." I remembered, she had two daughters; one in Kuwait, where, presumably, her first husband still lived, the other in the East (and Arab) side of Jerusalem.

"Are you close? Is she pleased to see you?"

"No."

"Not close? Or not pleased to see you?"

"Neither."

"Why not?"

"She is an Arab woman. She is married to a man who's very important politically. She is afraid of me. He would divorce her without a moment's hesitation if he knew she was a Jew."

"Doesn't he love her?"

A shrug.

"Why do you go to see her if she doesn't want you? Because she's your daughter? Do you love her very much?"

"Because of the boy."

"The boy? What boy?"

"It's an agreement. I keep out of her life. I don't go into her house, don't write to her, or call her. If she dies, she'll die without me. In return, once a week, I get the boy, her only child. We spend the afternoon together. I bring him back. Before the door opens, I'm already halfway down the street."

"Does he know you are Jewish?"

"Oh yes. He knows."

"Then he knows that he, too, is a Jew. Aren't you afraid he'll tell his father?"

"He doesn't know *he's* Jewish. Yet."

"But every five year old knows that if your mother is Jewish, you're Jewish too." The ancient sages were clever. Jewishness is transmitted through the female line only. It's a wise child that knows his own father.

"Every Jewish five-year-old. Not an Arab one. My grandson lives as an Arab."

"What do you talk about?"

"I talk to him about Jews."

"What do you tell him about Jews? Do you talk to him about yourself?"

"Everything."

I felt a strange sensation. I examined it. It was jealousy.

"But Rachel, why? Don't you see what conflicts it will bring him when he finally understands; within himself, with his world? Isn't it a cruel thing to do? Why don't you just leave it alone?"

Rachel scowled at me.

"He has to know."

She spoke with the sullen obduracy of a stupid woman. But Rachel was not stupid.

I didn't understand her at all. Then.

8. MAUTHAUSEN, 1943-5

I said, "Tell me about Mauthausen."
"You know all about Mauthausen. It was a Camp like all the others."
"I want to know what it was like for you. I want to see it through your eyes."
"Mine? Why mine? I was just a child whore. All I had was street knowledge. I knew that grown ups were either powerless to protect you or wanted to kill you. What did I know about life?"
"How was it in the Camp?"
"Hunger. We all had an obsession about food. I never thought of anything else. I dreamed about it. Caviare or raw cat flesh, any kind of food, it was all the same to me."
"Did you talk to the others?"
"What would we have talked about - going to the theatre, music? It was 1943 already. Germany had begun to feel the pinch. There wasn't much food to spare for the Camps. If we talked, it was about food.
"We waited for it all day. We smelt the soup, we felt the piece of bread crumbling in our fingers. From the moment we woke. Through the parade, the working day. Till it finally arrived. It was rationed out with scrupulous fairness by the kapos. Otherwise, we would have killed."
"Didn't you have a friend, a woman you could confide in?"
"To me they were all just hungry animals, like I was. I didn't see them as individuals."
"So you don't remember anyone special?"
"Oh yes, there was someone special. She changed my life."
A familiar stab of jealousy. "Is she still alive?"
"I killed her."
Rachel was speaking more freely than I had ever heard her, but for the first time, I felt the agitation under the tremendous control. Ashamed, I decided not to question her further, but, on her own volition, she continued.
"I worked in a munitions factory. Dangerous work. Poisonous vapours, many small explosions, our fingers were weak and cold and clumsy. Every time there was a mistake, someone got beaten or killed.

"We left the Camp very early in the morning. It was already dark, even in summer, when trucks brought us back. How many hours? We didn't count hours, we didn't count days. We huddled in the trucks, dreaming of food, then just dreaming, without hunger, and that was a sign of the end. Of 'natural' death, I mean. There were many other kinds.

"Some women ate. They were field workers, and as they picked, they ate - potatoes, beets, beans, cabbage, whatever it was. If they were caught, they were shot on sight. It didn't stop them. If it wasn't for their faces, you could almost have taken them for new arrivals. They had a bit of flesh on their bones.

"We slept on wooden boards, three to a shelf. In winter, we huddled close for warmth, stinking bags of bones. In summer, we tried not to touch. The stench was terrible.

"One of the women on my shelf was a field worker. She had been a year already in Mauthausen and she was still alive. She menstruated, even. She was on the outside, I was in the middle. Ours was the top shelf.

"This night she had diarrhoea. She was moaning and dripping over me. The smell, the sounds, the feel of her - I pushed her off the shelf. I was angry. Probably envious, too. She landed on the floor and the brittle bones cracked. She whimpered a bit, then stopped. I stretched myself out. I could bend my legs. What luxury! I could breathe. My hand touched two small roundish objects near where her head had lain. They were potatoes, probably meant for her sister, separated from her by chance in the next block. With great willpower, I crunched them very slowly, lying on my side. Then I turned on my back, relaxed and comfortable. I was in heaven.

"In the morning, the kapos got us to haul out her body, together with the others who had died during the night. Her sister came over. She screamed and flopped down and began to caress that dirty, smelly body, covered with flies, with the blood seeping out of the corner of its mouth and faeces seeping out at the other end.

"She held it in her arms and called it by its name, Lisa; the sister was called Ilse, I think. We never thought of each other as having names, just numbers.

"I saw with astonishment that to Ilse, Lisa wasn't just another animal which was now, as we all would be shortly, a dead animal, nothing remarkable. She was a human being with a distinct personality who had been loved. She was a unique, incomparable loss. All the others were unique, too. They were all human beings, and so was I. With this astounding discovery, came a sense of joy.

"They would not succeed in degrading me. They would not make me into an animal, the prey of the predators they were. I didn't believe, of course, in Gods and Spirits or Universal Knowingness, so I made a pact with myself. Whatever the circumstances, I promised myself to be always just what I was. If this is a faith, and it isn't, this is my faith. Myself, I think it's just a push in the behind from the Law of Survival.

"I looked after Ilse a bit. I couldn't get her food, but I gave her my place in the factory. It was under a window, so the slight breeze dissipated to some degree the poison-loaded air. In the truck, to and from work, I held her, so that the rough planks didn't jar her delicate, dissolving bones. The more she used up my new-found human feeling, the more I felt. She died, though. I mourned her. For her, for Lisa, I wanted to live.

"I believe it kept me going for a bit. But I was a bag of skin and bones. My eyes began to close, my mind began to drift, starvation took over and I knew I was starting to die. I didn't mind, mostly, of course, because of lethargy, but a small part of me now accepted death. I was dying as Rachel; not their prey, their number on my wrist.

"I didn't die, of course. We were liberated by the Americans. I was already very far gone, which was lucky, because those in better shape grabbed the chocolate bars, the candies, the tins of meat and condensed milk and meat loaf the shocked soldiers rushed to give them. Of course, it killed them, every one, their shrunken stomachs bloated like sheep in a field of alfalfa.

"I sat motionless, eyes vacant, mind floating: elsewhere. I frightened them, me and the others like me. By all accounts, I had really passed beyond the point of no return.

"I became briefly conscious, I don't know how long after, in a bed, a soft bed, which, after testing with my hand, I slowly realised I had all to myself. This was beyond all comprehension. I opened my eyes slightly and saw a bunch of people standing round me, mostly in white coats. I closed my eyes again. A man's voice said "kaput" in a sad sort of way. I realised they were talking about me. I opened my eyes again.

"Ich bin nicht kaput," I said in a disagreeable whisper. I thought I was shouting. A big black man came up close and looked at me. He said something I didn't understand. He spoke in English.

"I'm going to take on this one myself," he said.

9. ISRAEL, 1978

Avi called me early in the morning two days after we had met.
"Supermarket delivery service here. Need any tomatoes?"
"Oh, Avi!"
"Would you like to see a movie tonight? Do you like Westerns?"
I said, without thinking, "I can't stand them!" and then regretted it. But it was alright.
"I like an honest woman. How about old movies, Marlene Dietrich at the Cinemateque? Lubitsch 1932."
"That would be lovely."
"Should we eat first? About seven or so?"
"Oh Avi, I can't, I've got to work late. How about I meet you at the Cinemateque at eight?"
"Fine. See you then."
I then got very excited and tried on six different outfits before deciding on a skirt instead of my usual jeans, and a sleeveless white top that I could change into at the office.
Although all my usual nudniks were there, I sailed amicably through my day, even giving in on a couple of long and hotly contested battles - an extra food allowance ("for the children") to a woman I knew perfectly well had three sons who were all supporting themselves and "bus fare to the hospital" to an oldster in startling good health.
It was an unusually hot spring evening when I met Avi. A desert wind, the 'Khamsin', was blowing fine sand particles from the desert. He looked cool, though, in a short-sleeved shirt. The fading sun showed fine gold hairs on his arm, at odds with his otherwise rather dark colouring. They were oddly attractive.
The seats in the Cinemateque are on the skimpy side, and when we sat down, our arms were just touching. To my growing astonishment, instead of finding this contact only faintly distasteful (which is where I had got to after three years of psychoanalysis), it pleased me.
On an impulse, I leaned over to him and whispered, "Touch me."
Rather surprised, he took my hand.
"I'll tell my mother on you," he said. After a while, he shifted, and put his arm around me, with his fingers spread across my bare shoulder. And I liked that, too.

We had coffee, afterwards, at the Apropos. I had left my car parked outside the office because I didn't want to have to hunt for a parking place in central Tel Aviv, which more or less can't be found without the help of an astrologer or God. For the same reason, Avi hadn't brought his either, so he walked me home.

It was nearly midnight. "Can I come in, or are you one of these conventional girls that don't invite a man in until the second date?"

"I'm afraid so."

"In that case, do you mind if I sit down here for a couple of minutes?" He sat down forthwith on the stairs outside my door. Puzzled, I joined him. We didn't talk. After a bit he looked at his watch.

"It's five minutes past midnight which means it's tomorrow. We are on our second date. Now can I come in?"

I laughed and got up, opened my bag and took out my key.

"Come on in," I said.

It went a bit better than usual. I still liked it when he held me. I even liked his kisses, which was another first. But when we got into bed and he put his hand on my breast, I stiffened, as usual, and drew back, then bit my lip and consciously relaxed.

He withdrew his hand immediately.

"What's the matter?"

"Nothing. Go on."

"I can only make love to a willing woman. You don't want it, do you?"

A long pause. "Of course I do." I took his hand and put it back on my breast.

It lay there, immobile for a long time, then he put both hands behind his head.

I said, "Make love to me."

"No."

"You sound just like Rachel."

"What?"

"Nothing."

"Tell me, Gerda."

"There's nothing to tell."

"Tell me."

So I told him. The first man, not counting my analyst, I had spoken to about Uri. For some reason, even Tanta got into the act, all my hang-ups came pouring out.

He listened without interrupting, then he said: "We'll just wait until you're ready."

I said desperately, "We don't need to. I don't actually dislike it, I just don't much care for it. The psychoanalysis really helped me a lot. Please make love to me, I won't mind at all." I didn't want to lose him. I knew how important sex was to men.

I didn't know, then, that it was important to women, too.

He turned over, his back to me. "Go to sleep. We've both got work tomorrow. Don't worry about me, there are always cold showers. I'll wait."

I said, " It could take years."

"Try to settle for just a few decades. I'd like to be still capable."

Long afterwards, he told me he had thought it might take months.

In the event, it took all of ten minutes. I clung to him afterwards; I couldn't let him go.

"What are you, half woman, half octopus?" he grumbled, but he didn't detach himself, he was flushed and smiling and we slept the rest of the night in a hot and sticky tangle, both of us utterly relaxed.

I got up in the morning while he was still sleeping. I expressed my gratitude and love in a womanly way, which was in itself also new and unusual for me. I didn't generally bother about breakfast, I was a black-coffee-in-a-mug type. But I brought out the best china and dusted it off - the set I inherited from my mother, fine bone china decorated surprisingly with a palm tree and a hint of blue ocean. I made toast and wrapped it in a white napkin. I put the butter in a proper dish instead of leaving it in its packet. There was some smoked salmon left from Avi's expensive supermarket orgy and my cousin had brought me back from a trip a jar of Cooper's Oxford marmalade.

I made the coffee in a percolator, instead of spooning it direct into the cups (Israeli Army style: called 'botz' which means 'mud'. It actually isn't bad and that's how most of us make it even after our Service days). Then I woke him. He had a very quick shower, pulled on his pants, and came into the kitchen.

The table cloth was white. It looked quite dazzling because my kitchen gets the early morning sun. The coffee smell was fragrant.

He said, "Is this what everyone gets, or is it Special?"

"Special."

"Will I always get Special?"

"Always."

"Then I think I'll come again. Tonight I'm working late. How about to-morrow?"

"Yes."

"What do you want to do? A movie again? Or do you prefer a concert or a play?"

"To go to bed," I said.

I paid a visit, a couple of weeks later, to my analyst. I had stopped our weekly session two years ago. I didn't feel we were getting anywhere. I said, "Put away your receipt book. I'm not here as a patient. I just want some friendly advice."

"Who says I'm your friend? That will be fifty lirot."

I looked at him to see if he was serious, decided that he wasn't, and grinned. I told him what had happened, what was still happening, in my sexual life with Avi. I asked him: "Am I cured? Or will it come back?"

"Don't know."

"Is it just with Avi, or would it be alright with anyone?"

"Haven't the faintest idea."

"Oh Paul, don't be like that! Remember, you're just a friend."

"Tell you what, I've got Friday evening free between eight and ten. Come over and we'll find out." He gave me what he thought was a lecherous leer, but in his eyes were only caring and concern.

I laughed.

"What would you do if I said 'yes'?"

"Commit painless suicide before my wife got at me with an axe."

"Seriously, Paul, tell me what you think. I don't know what's happening to me." I used a Hebrew idiom. "I don't know how to eat it."

"Seriously, Gerda, neither do I. It could be a case of true love conquers all. Not very likely. It could have been sheer panic, a tremendous drive to maintain the relationship, or maybe because your body wants a child."

"I don't want a child."

"I didn't say 'you', Gerda, I said 'your body'."

"So you really can't tell me anything?"

"Come back to analysis. Maybe after half a year, we'll know."

I shook my head. "Thanks, Paul, but no. I'm going to fight it out in the real world, not on the couch."

"It doesn't make any difference, Gerda. The battlefield's in you. I just stir things up a bit, get them moving."

Again I shook my head. "They're already moving too fast for me; it scares me."

"Don't let it scare you. Life is good."

"Even with this Government?" Paul was vehemently left wing and so was I. The Government wasn't.

"In the midst of life we are in death," he quoted lugubriously. "Not everything has to be understood. Don't think about it. You're too cerebral. Have fun! Fuck your fellow till your balls drop off!"

I said with dignity, "I'm a woman. Women don't have balls."

"I told you from the start I wasn't a medical doctor. That'll be fifty lirot."

I looked at him again to see if he was serious, and this time he was. So I opened my purse and handed him a fifty lira note. He put it in his wallet.

"I thought we were just talking, like friends."

"I'm an analyst. I get paid for just talking. That's my trade. That's what I do. I don't do it for free."

It wasn't like him.

"What's eating you?"

Long pause. "Shit. I suppose I should tell someone. It's my wife. Every Friday afternoon we throw out the kids and go to bed. Just like the Religious, it's a mitzvah on a Friday. Very passionate, my wife. She makes a hell of a noise, groans, shouts, yells "don't stop," the works. Can't take her to a hotel without the neighbours thumping on the wall. This time, she just lies there. 'What's the matter, pet? Don't you feel well?'

"A start. 'Oh it's nothing. I was just thinking about something.'

"Begins to writhe and heave.

"I stop.

"'What were you thinking about?'

"Nervously, 'Nothing. Really. I was just wondering whether to roast the chicken tonight or to grill it.'

"My own fucking wife! I've been married to her for twenty years and never realised all the time she was faking it! Me! A professional! In the fucking trade! What am I to do now, I can't touch her."

I said, "Give yourself some time. That'll be fifty lirot."

"What?"

"I'm a social worker. I'm supposed to advise on family problems. That's what I do. I don't do it for free."

He grinned and handed me back my fifty lira note.

"Amazing - it really works! I feel better," he said.

In the ensuing weeks, Avi and I were together a lot, and we talked. I learned that Avi's parents came from Romania, but he and his brother were born in Israel, Sabras, like I was. I often thought he was rather dark for a Romanian. A bit of gypsy blood, perhaps, had infiltrated in at the grandmother level, or even further back. It wasn't unusual.

The family settled in Haifa, his father ran a bicycle repair shop, his mother worked in Ata, the textile factory (an Israeli legend) that had only recently closed. You couldn't compete with Korea and Taiwan. At one time, Ata underwear was worn by everyone, before it got fashionable, and people who were rich enough to go to London and buy up Marks & Spencer's, rumour had it buying Ata underwear there at twice the price under a different label.

Both had died some years previously, his father of cancer, his mother of a heart attack. Avi's older brother was also an engineer, and worked vaguely somewhere in Europe for the Common Market. Occasionally, he wrote.

Avi was a nut about automation and robotics. "Artificial Intelligence" he called it. He did all the research and development work for his small firm, which made electronic equipment for industry, and was now branching out into export.

Not long ago, they had sent Avi to visit a factory in the Midlands of England - Birmingham - to study the problems and needs.

"I spoke to a girl working on the factory line," he told me. "I asked her what she did.

"She said, 'I take this bit and I screw it into this other bit.'

"'That's all?'"

" 'Yup.'

"'What is it you are making?'"

"Silence.

" 'Dunno, Sir.'

"'What does the factory produce?'"

" 'Dunno.' "

Avi was savage about this. "No human being has to spend his life doing this sort of thing, stultifying, mindless, without any shred of satisfaction or goal. This, machines can do."

For Avi, his work was a major goal, just like for any genuine researcher. An obsession that overruled almost everything else. Most nights, he worked late at the lab.

10. MAUTHAUSEN (AFTER LIBERATION), 1945-6

I invited Rachel to the apartment for dinner. I wanted her to meet Avi. She accepted in principle, but couldn't fix a date. She said Professor Strumpfeld needed her now in the evenings. She would let me know. One evening, she phoned me. The professor's chess-playing friend was coming to spend the evening with him. They no longer played seriously: the friend sat, the Professor lay, in compatible silence.

"Get out," Professor Strumpfeld told her. "I've had enough of women! Leave me alone with Bernard to-night." He was not noticeably considerate now but neither did he take advantage.

I said to Rachel. "Great. Come over. Have dinner with us. Avi will be thrilled." This was not only a bit gushy, it wasn't even true. Avi was not thrilled.

"I'm sorry luv, but I have to work tonight."

"Oh, Avi!"

"I'll come home for dinner if you like, but afterwards I'll have to go back to the lab."

"Aren't you interested to meet her?"

"One woman's more than enough. Unless you insist. Do you insist I have a little bit on the side?"

I said, "Shut up," and punched him and we wrestled a bit. He was happy. I was sure he was happy with me.

I asked him to pick Rachel up on his way home from work. He drove an old Ford Escort, which shouldn't pose her the slightest difficulty.

They arrived. Why did I imagine there was some intimacy between them, from which I was excluded? As if they had shared some common experience that I had not? Avi wasn't a child of the Holocaust. His people apparently had come to Palestine themselves as children, and Avi was practically second generation Israeli. Like me, he was born here. What special link could he have with Rachel? They were so comfortable together, as if they knew each other's habits, language, a body language I didn't know at all.

I scolded myself for being fanciful. I served a beautifully prepared and elegant meal. We talked about quite ordinary things, cinema and music; politics of course. Although, as usual, Rachel was mostly silent, I couldn't throw off this obsessive feeling that they shared something that was foreign to me and of which I could never be a part.

Avi made his excuses straight after dinner and went back to the lab. He pleasantly told Rachel he had been delighted to meet her and hoped we would all soon get together again. Yet despite the proper formality, it was more as if he was saying 'au revoir' to a member of the family, a cousin; his cousin, not mine.

I was jealous, of course. But of whom? Of what?

Afterwards, Rachel helped me clean up. We lingered over another cup of coffee. She liked it thick, tiny, black and sweet, like an Arab. I indulged her, of course, but I drank 'botz', like an Israeli, a big cup of ground coffee with lots of milk.

The Italians drink it by the thimble. Of course, it's all Mediterranean.

On this evening, without any prompting on my part, Rachel told me about what happened to her after Mauthausen. Why did I feel that this was like a gift, a recompense, an apology for her exclusion of me with Avi? She made me this recompense with affection, but also with a trace of something else. Was it pity?

For months after her rescue from Mauthausen, Rachel lingered in and out of consciousness, probably at first more often out. What she remembered was a big black man, who seemed to her at times a saviour, at times a torturer.

He wouldn't leave her alone. He bullied her. In his execrable German, but growing more extensive, more fluent, even if still mispronounced, all the time, he told her she had to live. "Nicht kaput!" he would yell. "Nicht sterben!" "Mussen leben." "Mussen gesund sein." Sometimes he broke down into English. "Live, baby," he implored. "Live for me." "Live for good old Howard."

His name was Dr Howard Brock. It was unusual for a black physician to be assigned to a white unit in the American Army at that time, but then he wasn't a usual man. He had held a Professorship at Harvard Medical School. His area of expertise was diseases of malnutrition. He was an expert of high international standing.

He was about sixty, a widower, grown-up children all doing well. He had the rank of Colonel and was greatly respected.

"It seemed to me that whenever I was conscious, he was there. He pulled me into consciousness. I resented it. The not-being was so effortless, so sweet. He talked at me, endlessly, on this single theme, I had to live. I was drip fed glucose, but after a time, he began to gently slap me awake, and when I was, he would put a piece of sponge into my mouth.

" 'Close your lips and suck it, damn you. Suck it!' "

"I didn't want to. I wished he would go away, but it was less effort to do what I was told. 'Good girl.' But then there would be another piece of sponge between my sore gums. 'Go on, suck it, fucking well suck it, you bitch.' So I sucked.

"He fixed a mirror on the bottom of my bed. The head nurse was astonished.

" 'What the hell is that for? If she sees herself she'll scare herself to death.' "

" 'It's not angled so that she can see herself. It's angled to show her the window, the trees, the birds. People passing. We've got so little, we have to use all we've got.'

"I can't tell you how good that was!

"Then he began to give me rewards. If I sucked three sponges, he played me music.

"He had a gramophone, and lots of the short play records there were at that time. He liked classical music. He had Bach and Mozart and Vivaldi.

"The sponges got replaced by spoonfuls, very carefully, one at a time, at shorter and shorter intervals. Where did he find the patience, the time? He must have had other patients. Did he ever sleep? He was always there for me. I got talked about. 'Dr Brock's Special'. There were stories about me floating around. At one time I had bedsores, ulcers, infections. He got hold of a metal worker and made him cut a circular hole in the bed where the sores were. 'Got to take the pressure off,' he told an outraged Matron. He had penicillin. If he got it on the black market, it must have taken all of his colonel's pay.

"Another time, I felt something damp between my legs. He was sitting beside me. He was as quick as a ferret. He pulled back the sheet and gave a great shout. A nurse came running. 'She crapped,' he yelled exultantly, 'she crapped!'

"As I improved, he told me stories, half in German, half in English. I recognised them, they were children's stories, my mother had told me them before I could read. Mostly, the Sleeping Beauty, over and over again.

"Then, mushes and gruels. Finally, getting out of bed. Sitting in a chair. He never let me look at myself in the mirror. 'It's a tree mirror,' he said."

11. ISRAEL, 1979

Recently, I had had a love affair (how I hate the word 'relationship'!) with an Australian fellow, a forty-year old physicist - never been married, always a risk. 'Sandy', he was called. He was a decent enough man, not very handsome, eyes too little, black hair too curly and exuberant, I suppose too feminine for my taste, I could have got used to it. The real problem, though, was, I suppose, a throwover from being a scientist; he wanted perfection.

He wasn't very tactful about it; we would be sitting together, drinking coffee at some street café, Rowal was our favourite even though it was expensive, the coffee was so good.

"Look at that woman!" he would exclaim. "Hasn't she got a marvellous figure? That's the sort of figure I like."

I would look hopelessly at some model who probably existed on coffee and dry toast and amphetamines, dressed in a wisp of black nothing that exposed perfect full oval breasts practically to the nipples.

"Why don't you go on a diet?" he would ask.

My smile wasn't as warm and rich as Greer Garson's, my eyebrows as exquisitely shaped as Marilyn Monroe's. I couldn't iron shirts like his mother. I didn't have style like the woman next door. I don't mean that he was always critical. He praised the qualities he thought I did have, generously. It was just he wanted it all. Even in bed.

"You would look terrific with black hair. Could you dye your hair? I love your breasts. They're so soft. Maybe they could be just a little bigger. Try exercises, it might help."

How furiously I resented this. I was my own woman, not something to be made over to please his - or anybody's - special tastes.

He had no idea what he was doing to me. It wasn't that I couldn't bear the criticism. But my own self-image was already so low, I was afraid these rough winds might crash it down to nothing at all. I was so obviously not 'right' for him, I was afraid I would lose him. Perversely, this made me want to lose him and get it all over with: so I would compile, silently, my own list of his deficiencies; the curly hair (I didn't like curly hair); the inability to listen, to me or anyone else; liking Jerry Lewis films; always wanting to be right, and telling you when he was. "Do I really like him at all?" I would wonder, and then he would do something heart-stopping, like putting his head in my lap and telling me how much he needed me.

I used to talk about him to my cousin.

"Why do you mind so much?" she asked, amused. "You know you can't be perfect, not just 'perfect', for him, but for anyone, just as he can't be perfect for you. He evidently doesn't understand that - if he did he wouldn't be a forty-year-old bachelor. But he'll learn. Slowly. As long as he doesn't beat you for not being a seventeen-year-old Twiggy who probably would bore him to tears in a week. Can you see him sitting there at a rock session or listening to a detailed account of her diet? He just dreams. Let him."

I said, "I think I mind because it's always the packaging - the size of the box, the shape, the colour of the wrappings. He doesn't care about the valuable things, the things inside. Not how I look. Me! What I am."

"Gerda, you're complaining about the difference between men and women. You can't take on evolution. Why don't you just become a lesbian?"

I looked a bit shocked, so she laughed, and hugged me. "Men! They're so awful and we need them so much."

She said, "Don't 'pay him back. Don't be destructive! It's just pinpricks."

But I did 'pay him back'. I told myself I had to teach him a lesson, but it wasn't, it was pure revenge.

"I wish your hair was straight," I said, playing with it, tugging gently at the superfluity of glossy curls. "You look like one of the Muppets with this mop. Straight hair is manly. Like Marlon Brando." "I really like a tall man," I said. He was 5ft 6 inches and quite slim; he wore glasses. "Big men make me feel so protected."

I nibbled away at him, and was savagely glad when he tried to please me, combing his hair and smothering it with oil till it stuck out in straight spikes and felt like jelly. I gave him no credit. "Now you look like a porcupine," I said, and went to fetch a towel to wipe my hands. The more he made these pathetic endearing gestures, the more I revelled in my triumph, the more he was devalued in my eyes.

Of course it was a disaster, coming quickly to its inevitable conclusion. In pace with my destruction of his self-confidence - which probably wasn't much greater than mine, and infinitely more essential and vulnerable - we became more distant, more considerate and polite, turning ourselves into strangers. The time between meetings became longer and longer, and they were fixed by appointment, instead of just turning up. Going to bed became mechanical, then embarrassing, then a failure. We began just to meet for coffee and a chat. Then I saw him, at our Rowal, with his head close to another woman. There was no mistaking the intimacy of those almost touching hands.

She was entirely unexpected. In my arrogance I still thought of him as mine. She was about as far from a seventeen-year-old Twiggy as you could get. Thirty was long behind her, and perhaps even forty, I suspected. She would find it difficult to get into a size 48, in fact she was hovering on 'extra large'. She was blonde, with an attractive wide mouth and a heart-warming smile. She wasn't blowsy, more motherly, I suppose. From her glazed eyes, the way she exposed the tip of her tongue, her body gestures, the way her eyebrows rose in surprise, it was clear she thought him the most brilliant, entertaining, sexiest man in the world. Either that, or she was Sara Bernhardt.

He married her within six weeks, two children, widow's pension and all, and I would bet that she replied to all his disparaging remarks and comparisons with an affectionate, cheerful, "Yes, dear," in perfect unconcern and no hurt feelings at all. She knew what she was. I envied her.

When I told Evelyn all this, she only said, "Describe her to me."

"I told you. She's built, heavy, luscious, big breasts, big everything, talks a lot, very animated, tells jokes, has everybody laughing, they love her, nice kids, polite, intelligent. I hear she's a gourmet cook, not a stupid woman either, got a degree in Middle Eastern history, keeps a nice house."

"Now tell me what you're like."

"Well, I've got mousy brown hair, not any particular colour really. Small eyes, also no particular colour, sort of muddy grey with brown flecks. A brownish-greyish woman. Hands and feet are all right, but my bottom's like my mother' - sticks out, English, big, lumpy; I've got her skin too, slightly pocked, like a chicken's. I would be greatly improved if I lost about 5kg, especially around the waist and chin. Over sensitive and under-educated in the things that matter." I paused for a moment and then added, "and I'm a slob."

"I see a delicate honey-blonde, straight gleaming hair with gentle curves, a soft body, unusual eyes, pale green flecked with gold, like sunlight seen through a grove of ferns. Substantial, not a dream, firm body, a real armful of real woman. Beautifully shaped breasts. Clever, charming; and modest, too."

"Oh Evelyn! That isn't me!"

"It isn't you as you see yourself. That's your problem! You need so much reassurance, more than most men could possibly manage. If only you could learn to like yourself a bit more."

This problem never arose with Avi. I don't know how he saw me, but whatever it was, it was enough, he wanted no more. It was infinitely restful, and it was something I recognised. I think it was what my mother had looked for, too, and found in my father, after a long search, after everyone had assumed she was 'on the shelf' for good. A man who was content.

Once I asked Avi, we were in bed, our love-making had been satisfying, we were tired and close, ready to be confidential;

"Avi, isn't there anything about me you want to change?"

"Nope."

"Wouldn't you like me to be more beautiful?"

"Nope. You'd only spend hours looking at yourself in the mirror. It would take you a century to get dressed. We'd miss the beginning of every play or movie and I'd never understand what they were all about. We'd always miss the first course and I'd never get to eat smoked salmon or snails. I'd loathe you."

"Richer?"

"Certainly not. Rich people only like other, even richer people. You'd leave me for a heroin dealer or a Mafia prince."

"Sexier?"

"Good God, no! You've made me an old man already. I'm exhausted. I'm worn out before my time."

I moved my hand experimentally. "Not too old," I said.

Avi asked me, "Seriously. Is there anything about me you'd like different?"

"Oh yes. Your position. I don't like you so much flat on your back. I like to look straight up at you." He obliged.

Later, I said, "Sandy wanted me different." (I had told him about Sandy; I think I had told him about everything that had ever happened to me and nearly everything I felt about it).

"Sandy's a scientist. It's his job to change things and see what happens when you do. I'm just an engineer. If it works on the seventh day, you rest. I tried once, after I got a machine just right, to design it to be even better. When I got it to run faster, it got more expensive; when I got it cheaper, it broke. When I got it smaller, you couldn't repair it easily and so on. Then one of the older chaps taught me the First Law of Engineering - if it works, have a beer and leave it alone. You can't change one thing properly without changing some other, and then you're back to the drawing-board. Even if you could get it perfect in every way, by the time you got there, some other bugger would have his version in production already."

Of course, love affairs ('relationships', you just can't avoid that word), aren't static. There is a curve in the affairs of men and women. Ours seemed to go always up. Slowly, but up. I noticed that Avi was beginning to stop bothering to use a condom. Was he less afraid of an 'accident', which might spell out a serious involvement, or had he just begun to trust me more? Next, plans became more long-term and at the same time more communal.

"We really ought to buy a new bed."

'We', not 'you' as it would certainly have been a few months ago. Before that, it would never have come up at all - my bed was my business.

Then, "Do you think we might go abroad next spring?"

Next spring? It was hardly yet winter. All pretence of living in his own room went by the board. I didn't know if he was still paying rent on it, but all his belongings moved to my apartment.

Once, he said, "Do we really need two cars?"

It seemed to me that these were the first shoots of permanence, that would blossom into "Let's get married," or "Let's have a child."

Then we bloody well did. I was tidying my odds and ends in the toiletry cupboard one Saturday morning - not so much out of a spirit of order as because I had just been given a present of a huge jar of Yardley's Lavender Hand Cream, my favourite of favourites, and I needed to make room for it - when I noticed an unopened packet of Tampax. "That's odd," I thought, remembering I had bought it when I ran out. It seemed a long time ago. I made a quick rough calculation. It was probably six weeks. I tried to remember when I last had my period and that seemed, too, to be rather far back. I checked my pills. There were far too many. A bit disturbed, I thought I'd just run a check in the morning.

My gynaecologist at the Clinic is a cheery red-faced Romanian, who looks like a butcher, as all good gynaecologists do. He knows me well. He examined me, straightened up, took off his gloves, and said. "Congratulations. I hope it's a boy."

"Oh my God! How long?"

"Oh, about seven weeks I would say, possibly eight. Didn't you know? Didn't you have any symptoms? No morning sickness? No urgent desire for a pickled cucumber dipped in chocolate at three o'clock in the morning?"

"Nothing," I said, "nothing at all."

"You're lucky," gloomily. "So's your young man. With my wife, it's worse than acute cerebral malaria. Every time. What's it to be? Book you at the hospital, or an abortion?"

"I'll let you know."

"Don't make it too long. Come back in a couple of days."

"Thanks, Reuben."

"For nothing. Good luck."

That night, I told Avi. I was anxious, regretful, pleased and not pleased. I wanted the baby. I wanted to hear, I thought I might hear, the magic words. But I didn't want him to think I had trapped him, purposefully, or even negligently , although I suppose I had. So I told him, in detail, about tidying up and what the doctor said and that it was Avi's choice. Avi went very white. Then he put on his coat that he had just taken off - he was only just back from work.

"Where are you going?"

"Out."

"It's raining."

"I won't be long. I have to think. I'll come back."

"Do you promise?"

"I promise."

He didn't come back for three hours, during which time I began to put the food back in the refrigerator, then stopped, and threw myself on the bed and cried. He stood at the foot of the bed and looked at me.

"You're a mess," he said, neutrally, not nastily. Red eyes and swollen cheeks. Straggly hair. I suppose I was.

12. MAUTHAUSEN (AFTER LIBERATION), 1946

"It was a field hospital, they had set it up next to the Camp, in the middle of a field. It was green all around, and there was a small wood nearby. Dr Brock got them to put up a sort of veranda, it was for all the patients. The time came when he used to sit me out there on a padded chair for a few hours every day. It was pretty. I didn't speak much. I couldn't read. It was enough, though. New sensations filled me. He still made up all my food himself, nearly always he still fed me. Left to myself, I would take a few spoonfuls, then lose interest. The nurses were too busy. Nearly every day, someone died or nearly died. He was at me all the time. "Die Floegelach," he said, still in atrocious German.

"Didn't you talk to the other patients?"

"You don't understand. Most of the time I wasn't there. I wasn't broadcasting. I was just a receiver. I took things in. I gave nothing out. There was only a body, a body with no needs, that just obeyed.

"Suddenly, I changed. From indifferent, I became ravenously hungry. He was very pleased, but he didn't change my food. He still rationed me, measured all my meals. I couldn't understand why he wouldn't let me eat. I tried to gobble from my plate and he took it away from me. He forced me to eat slowly, a pause between each spoonful. It was still gruels and soup. I dreamed of solid food - he wouldn't let me touch it.

"Once a soldier visiting someone in the ward gave me a chocolate bar, a Mars bar I think it was called. I hid it under my pillow. I thought I would eat it at night when he wasn't there.

"He had X-ray eyes. He pulled it out. He was immediately terribly angry. 'You stupid ass-hole, you moron,' he shouted. 'Don't you know this could kill you?' Tears rolled down my cheeks. I wasn't upset by his incomprehensible anger. I was mourning the loss of my chocolate bar.

"A nurse came up. She understood the situation immediately. 'Don't scold her,' she said. 'She's only a kid.' He calmed down and suddenly his face twisted.

"'Just a kid who wants a chocolate bar,' he said. 'Just a kid.' He took out a pocket knife and unwrapped the bar. He cut off a slice, a very thin slice, and gave it to me. He put the rest in his pocket. He cut me off a slice every day.

"There were set-backs of course, but I got better. I don't have a clear idea of time, but I remember incidents.

"The day he put me on to solid food. He watched me. He had no sense of convention, of the proprieties. He watched me excrete, he examined, he even weighed my shit.

"Soon after this, I began to walk about. The walks got longer. I walked over to the Camp. It had changed completely. There were tents and huts, campbeds with pillows and blankets, even sheets. The barbed wire had gone. Soldiers were around, American soldiers. They were friendly. The gate stood open. Why didn't everyone go?

"I spoke to a girl of, I guess, about my age. It was sometimes hard to tell. 'Why don't you go?'

" 'Go where?' "

"Home, of course."

"She said, 'Where might that be?' "

"Someone else explained. She went back to Cologne, her hometown. There was a family she didn't know living in her parents' house. They wouldn't talk to her. They told her to go away. She recognised some of the neighbours, but there were mostly new faces. No-one would talk to her. There were no Jews left.

"It was like being in a parallel world; like passing through a time warp. It was the same in some ways, there was the school, the town hall, the railway station, in other ways it was totally different. It was a place with which she had no connection. She came back to the Camp.

"Some of the Polish Jews left and didn't come back. They were massacred by the Poles."

I asked Rachel: "Didn't you want to go back? Back to your home. Just to see it?"

"I never thought about myself. My whole existence was so fragile. I didn't react even to other people's experiences. I listened. Some things I understood, others I didn't. It didn't matter.

"I had a cough, which worried Dr Brock. More penicillin. My food regime began to catch up with my hunger. I could eat anything, small quantities, but real food, meat and chicken and potatoes. Even chocolate.

"Then one day, I didn't get any lunch. I said to a nurse: 'Where is Dr Brock? Why am I not getting my meal?' "

" 'Food?' she asked. 'Why don't you go down to the dining room? It's self-service. Help yourself.'

"'But, Dr Brock ..... ?'

" 'You'll find him there. He eats too, you know.' "

"Being able to choose my own food, to eat whatever and as much as I liked, was joy and terror. I didn't know how to function in such freedom, without direction, having to make my own rules. I had no will. I knew I had survived, and I had survived as Rachel, a person. But who was Rachel?

"One day, Dr Brock took me for a walk in the woods - he often took me for walks. He spent less time with me now, he had other patients. He didn't sit by my bed, but he still saw me every day; he examined me as a physician but he also talked a lot to me, in a garble of English and German, as a friend. That day, he suddenly stopped and held me by both my arms.

"He said, 'We did it! You're a girl, Rachel. You're a beautiful young girl again. Do you know that? Have you looked at yourself lately? You're just like any very pretty, normal teenage girl.'

"And I forgot. I was so full of gratitude! I wanted to give him something. What did I have to give? So I lifted up my skirt and said, 'There's nobody around. You can have it now if you want.'

"He took one look and turned his head and walked away. I thought perhaps he was shy. I was sure he'd come at night. I took a special, long, bath. I borrowed some perfume from one of the nurses, I got into bed and waited for him to come."

"And did he?"

"No. He shot himself. On the way back to his room one of the other doctors greeted him. 'Hi, Brock,' and he looked at him and said, 'They always win. You think you've beaten them but in the end they always win.' His colleague thought he was talking about a local army football match. A few minutes later, he heard a shot.

"It was all hushed up. 'Accident' of course. Cleaning his gun. He never touched a gun."

"Did he leave you a note?"

"All he left me was his GI insurance money."

"How did you hear about it?"

"In the morning. One of the other doctors sent for me. He looked at me coldly, suspiciously, I thought.

" 'Dr Brock's dead,' he said, 'I'll be looking after you now. He left you some money, by the way.'

"I went straight to Matron who had always been friendly, and she told me about it. 'Such a nice man! Everybody liked him. It made no difference him being black. Superb doctor, too, never knew anyone like him. So devoted. I can't imagine what could have upset him, you were doing so well, he was so proud of you. A great loss.'

"I screamed and howled. I wouldn't dress, or comb my hair. I wouldn't eat. Punishment, of course. They didn't know how to handle me. I lay in bed with my eyes closed. But I was thinking, at last.

"'What sort of a person are you?' I asked myself. I wasn't a child. I knew I would never be a whore again. Who was I?

"I was devastated. I was out of control. They gave me sedatives. I was too busy to eat. I had to become someone, I had to bridge the years I never had. I couldn't ever make a mistake like that again."

"Did you think about your childhood?"

"That, too."

"What were your parents like?"

"Papa? I think he thought he was a new model of Paul Ehrlich. He tried to be like him. He was a heart surgeon. Very well-known. Very respected. The nurses, everyone, 'Ja, Herr Professor.' 'Selbstverständlich, Herr Professor!' Cigars, very hearty, slap on the back to a colleague, reassuring - his patients were always certain they'd get well. They mostly didn't, of course. In those days. Very into German philosophy, German Kultur, read Nietzsche, quoted him all the time. Played Tannhauser on his gramophone when a patient didn't survive. He was the son of a Rabbi. You'd never have guessed! Didn't want to know. Small contribution to the Jewish orphanage, plant a tree in Palestine. Bigger ones to the German Nature Protection Society, Leipzig Opera Fund, and so on. Despised Polish Jews. Thought the Nazis had a point. Not him, of course. He was German."

"And your mother?"

"I don't think she was even Jewish at all. Some mystery about her family. No-one ever visited. There were phone calls very occasionally. She would shut the door. Afterwards, a flushed face. I think probably she came from an aristocratic German family, 'von Something'. They cut her off. After she thumbed her nose at them and ran away to marry her Jew. Mitigating circumstances, though. At least he looked like a gentleman! So a phone call, every now and then."

"What was she like?"

"Oh, a cultured German lady. Concerts, theatre, opera. Tea parties with colleagues' wives. Very dignified, very much 'Frau Professor'. Doilies under the tea cups. Servants who were taught to curtsey."

"Anyone else?"

"Yes, my grandmother. On my father's side. The Rabbi's widow. Very devout. Insisted on prayers before meals, Sabbath observance, candles - my father couldn't stand it. Couldn't stand her at all, for that matter!

"So they found a solution; she ate alone. Had meals in her own room, special kosher food. They almost never invited her down. Birthdays, and of course, at Christmas, when she wouldn't come.

"My mother had dresses made for her, little old lady dresses, in case anyone met her on the stairs. She wouldn't wear them. She had old, stiff, black long dresses from Poland, with a shawl, and head coverings. The Rabbi's wife.

"I often sat with her. She told me stories. She read to me, too, religious books, but also stories about Jewish history: the Exodus from Egypt; the building and destruction of the First and Second Temples; the Maccabees; the Exile; the Inquisition, the sword-makers of Toledo. She showed me pictures of Palestine. The barren hills. The kibbutzim. She told me I must not forget Jerusalem, for two thousand years Jews had not forgotten Jerusalem.

"I didn't even know where it was! But I believed her. I knew I mustn't forget; otherwise, the world would come to an end!

"I did forget though. For a time. But after Dr Brock died, after I killed him, I remembered Jerusalem. I remembered my grandmother more than anyone else. I believed that perhaps my having forgotten Jerusalem had brought about the end of my world."

"What happened to her?"

"Luckily for her, she died in a train accident. She had gone to visit her sister. In 1940, before things got really bad."

"Did you go to her funeral?"

"No. There was an argument. 'She has to have a Jewish funeral, she has to be buried next to her husband,' my mother said.

"Her husband, after Poland, had been the rabbi of a small community in Mecklenberg where my father was born.

" 'It's not proper any other way.' 'Proper' was one of her favourite words.

"My father objected. 'We can't afford to be conspicuous.' So in the end, they shipped her body to her sister in Mecklenberg, along with a cheque. None of us went.

"She was his mother, but after she was killed, my father breathed relief in every pore. They made her room into a library. German literature. My father was beginning to be afraid, I think.

"Then the roof fell in. He was too prominent. They dismissed him from the hospital. Former colleagues didn't want to know him. He wasn't allowed to practise, even among the Jews.

"He went to the local Nazi Party Headquarters. 'But I'm a German,' he said. 'My uncle died fighting for Germany in the War.' (It wasn't World War I yet - just 'the War'). They laughed and kicked him out. Literally. He had bruises on his back. He had to wear a yellow star. So did she. I think my father tried to send her back to her family, but they wouldn't have her. The phone calls stopped. The maids left, too. It wasn't allowed. They sent me away to a cousin in a smaller town; they thought it would be safer. Or could they not stand their daughter witnessing their humiliation? They hardly went out. Just at night for food. It wasn't safe. They half-starved, their German Kultur all around them; the books, the gramophone records, old programmes of 'approved' concerts and plays. A German life.

"Then the police came. They were told to each pack a small bag. They were put into the cattle trucks, they were gassed, they went to their Jewish deaths, Germans to the last.

"I often wonder what their last words were to each other.

"'Oh Ernst! I've forgotten my pearls!'

"'Never mind, darling, I'll get you a new string.'

"'But they were the family pearls; from Tante Tilda. You don't understand.'

"'We'll send for them. The neighbours will send them on.'

"He knew, of course. He wasn't a fool. She went naked to her Jewish death, like all the rest."

I had been thinking. I said carefully:

"If your mother wasn't Jewish, according to religious law, to Halacha, then you aren't Jewish either, you know."

She looked at me. "What does Halacha know about who is a Jew? The Germans knew. Who could challenge their definition?. They put their mark on me as a Jew."

"But, legally?" I insisted.

A rueful smile. "I thought of that, too. When I was finding out who I was, I never doubted I was a Jew; if I had not been one, they had made me one, I was entitled. Still, to absolve any doubts, I got myself converted."

"You converted to Judaism?"

"Yes, later in Switzerland. It was just a formality, though. I was already a Jew."

"So you didn't eat?"

"I told you. I couldn't eat. I was unmanageable. It went on for a long time. They drugged me. They were worried, they didn't know what to do with me. It wasn't loving-worried, like with Dr Brock. It was doing-a-job worried. They got a psychologist to 'look at' me.

"He talked to me a few times. He told them it was beyond his experience, he didn't understand me at all. There wasn't anything to understand. I was nothing."

"So what did they do?"

"I began to cough, and my sputum tests were positive. I was very thin. They sent me to a sanatorium in Switzerland. On his GI money. They were glad to get rid of me. It seemed a good solution.

"I didn't want to go. They told me I'd die if I didn't. I looked at them with amazement. So what?

"But they packed me into a train, with a nurse; and then a cog wheel mountain train, and the Sanatorium took over.

At first, I was kept very busy. X-rays, tests, weighings, temperature, I didn't care, then a long period when I was not allowed to talk, hardly to move. That suited me. During that time, some things fell into place. I was a Jew. My grandmother had not taught me to be a Jew, the Germans had. But she had made it a viable option. She gave me a choice. I learned there were choices. I decided I wanted to live. I became docile. I began to eat. As I got better, they let me read a bit.

"Swiss sanatoriums at that time were unbelievably strict. If you didn't do what you were told, you got slung out. It was a rich person's sanatorium, people from everywhere, France, England, America, mostly young. Herr Director was youngish. All-powerful; like my father."

13. ISRAEL, 1979

Dr Lustig had taken to visiting the Professor rather frequently. Dr Lustig was also a man living on his own, his wife having died a few years previously. They had no children; or so I thought. Until he told me casually one day he would be leaving early, as he was going up to Jerusalem to see his son.

"I didn't know you had a son."

"Actually, I have a son and a daughter. My daughter isn't in Israel, though. Lives in France."

"I'm glad you have the boy here. Is he married? Do you have grandchildren?" I thought he'd make a wonderful grandfather. He was kindly and he had the directness, the perception of what mattered and what didn't to a child.

Drily: "Hardly. He's a priest."

"So what? Rabbis have dozens of kids. It's a 'mitzveh'. Especially on Friday nights."

"I didn't say he was a rabbi. I said he was a priest, a Catholic priest. In fact, he's the abbot of the Franciscan Monastery and before you ask, ironical as it might sound, my daughter also took her holy vows - she's in a nunnery in France, nursing order, expects to be sent to Zambia next year. Martyr type."

I said, "Oh!" My face was very red.

"Don't be embarrassed. I suppose it is a bit of a personal sorrow, you hope to have your kids around you in your old age. We left our two with a very devout Catholic family, friends, in Germany. They were risking their lives. After a time, it got unsafe, so they put the boy in a monastery and the girl in a nunnery, both in France, teaching orders, with boarding pupils. My daughter was only four years old when we left her. She still thinks she's a true-born Catholic, nobody disillusioned her. It was less dangerous that way. The boy knows, he was seven. What do you expect; the only parents he knew were the monks. The couple who took them were killed in the bombing, we couldn't find them. Nobody knew where the kids were, we searched for years.

"Then, by chance, we found Paul, he was seventeen by then and in a seminary. There was another kid, also a Jewish convert, also from Berlin. There are a lot of them, you know. They recognised each other, they had been schoolmates. This other kid left the seminary, found he had an aunt still alive, went to live with her, reverted to being a Jew. He put us on to Paul and Paul knew about his sister.

"We corresponded for a bit. He said he respected us with filial love, not much of it that I can see; he was totally devoted to Christ. Did well, you know. Abbot at thirty-seven years of age, almost unheard of. Been in Jerusalem about two years now. Visits me once a month. I visit him on feast days. Nothing to say to each other, though: 'hope you're well' and that's about that. Sometimes he tries to save my soul from eternal damnation and urges me to adopt the True Faith. It's odd to hear that from your own kid. I used to play Chanukah games with him, taught him a bit of Jewish history, too.

"I remember his mother wrote a little Purim play, just to put on for a few friends - he was King Ahasuerus, my girl was Queen Esther. She couldn't remember her lines of course, but she looked sweetly pretty; white dress, gold cardboard crown.

"I don't bother her. There's no point. I try not to get into religious arguments with the boy. You know me, I'm a secular Jew. If I don't believe in the Jewish God I'm certainly not going to believe in the Catholic one. Yes, I love the boy, of course I love him, he's my son. I just can't stand the sight of him."

At this point Dr. Lustig turned away from me. I got out fast.

In this country, there's a story under every stone.

He told me now that Professor Strumpfeld's period of remission had slowly ended. He felt very tired, dizzy, fainted a couple of times, had no appetite, the blood count wasn't good at all.

Rachel, Dr Lustig told me, made him a French dish that had thirty-seven ingredients and took two days to prepare. To him, it tasted like straw. Of course he didn't tell her, shoved down the lot. But she knew. The next day and following that there were simple custards, easy to get down.

The doctors decided to take strong measures, radiation and chemotherapy; they wanted to hospitalise him for a couple of weeks. Refused point blank, said he would take the treatment, would come up to the Hadassah Hospital in a taxi, but at night he was going to sleep in his own bed.

He told Dr Lustig how it was, afterwards. The treatment did do him good. He was a bit livelier. But his complexion was grey already, he had almost no flesh on his bones, it wasn't going to be many months.

"I went with Rachel in a taxi to Jerusalem, to the hospital. I wanted to go by myself. She said she could use a day in Jerusalem, if I didn't mind. She was lying in her teeth. She never left me. I was told some people have only minor side effects, with others it could be severe. I was fairly sure that with me it would be severe. It hit me in the taxi going home. I began to have paroxysms of vomiting. I felt like death. The driver complained about the mess in the car."

'I won't be able to take another passenger. It stinks to hell in here!'

"Rachel opened her purse and took out a hundred lira note. She tore it in half and gave him one half. 'This is for cleaning the car. You'll get the other half when we get back provided from now on you don't open your mouth.' He didn't say a word. Turned out she'd come with a couple of packs of Kleenex. Cleaned me up. Each time."

"I said to her, 'This can't be very pleasant for you.'"

"A shrug. 'I've seen worse.'"

"When we got home, she put me to bed. I was so weak I couldn't have managed to undress. Sponged me under the shower, too. A job. Like cleaning the toilet. Some jobs are better than others, but it's all just work. I found that tolerable.

"I was still vomiting. She held the basin. She wiped my face. It began to wear off a bit. I may have dozed. I looked up, she was standing beside the bed, holding out a book.

" 'I'm glad you woke. It's time for my Hebrew lesson.'

"'Your what?'

"'My Hebrew lesson! It's four o'clock. In fact, we're five minutes late.'

"'Rachel, you can't expect me to give you a Hebrew lesson in this state!'

"I vomited again. 'See?'

"She said: 'We agreed.' She washed out the basin, but she came back, still with the book. She wasn't going to give in.

"Strangely enough, when she said 'It's five o'clock. We can stop now.' I had forgotten about the chemotherapy. I hadn't vomited once. She had got me into a complicated argument on the origin of some words. I felt a hell of a lot better. That's how it went all the time. Four o'clock she was there with her book, I told her I wasn't up to it, she insisted and afterwards I felt more or less over it all. At least, I felt like myself, not just a sick old man, useless, worthless, defiled. She's a remarkable woman, you know."

Dr Lustig knew. He clutched the Professor's now rather fragile hand. "Auf Wiedersehen."

The Professor grinned and said, "Ciao." Dr Lustig found his way down to the kitchen. Rachel was drinking coffee. She made him a cup.

"He's not going to get any better. A couple of months at most, you know."

"I know."

"You're doing a great job. He likes you. You're a great help to him. He's probably not going to get out of his bed again. He'll need changing his pyjamas, turning, heavy going. Can you manage?"

"Yes."

"Not too much for you emotionally? I'm sure you're attached to him."

"Everybody dies."

"Still getting your Hebrew lessons?"

"As long as he can." A smile.

14. SWITZERLAND, MAUTHAUSEN (AFTER LIBERATION), 1946-7

"Tell me again. What was it like at the Sanatorium?"
"Like school. Rules. Permitted behaviour. Punishment. Reward."
"Not like a hospital?"
"Not at all like a hospital. Medical examination, of course. I was positive. So bed rest. A room to myself, like in a hotel. I was hardly allowed to speak. No books at first. Music, though. The Director believed in music. Every day they wheeled my bed on to the balcony. The mountains were so beautiful. Everything was so still."
"Did it worry you that you were sick?"
"I didn't care. I wasn't sure I wanted to live. I just wanted to think about it. It was an ideal place."
"And then?"
"When my sputum was negative, they let me get up. I went to the dining room for meals. I met the other patients."
"What were they like?"
"Conversations were not encouraged, they weren't part of the cure."
"Who were they?"
"Mainly young people. Children of the rich. From many countries. There was an English boy, I remember, he told me he got sick because there wasn't much food in Britain during the War.
"'What did you eat?' I asked him.
"'We got monthly rations. We *starved*! Two eggs a week, a couple of ounces of butter, six ounces of sugar, hardly any meat, except whale meat. Milk, of course. Bread and baked goods were on 'points'. Hardly any fruit. That was all.'
"It sounded like Paradise to me.
"'Even restaurant meals cost 'points'.'
"'You had restaurant meals?'
"'Well, of course! Not very good, mind you. Still, one shouldn't complain. Expect you had rationing too.'
"I didn't know how to talk to them. So I didn't. Besides, they thought I was a German."

"Did they hate the Germans?"

"I think they rather admired them. Still, they were the enemy. I made them uncomfortable."

"After six months I was still negative and I was allowed to go into town. With permission each time, of course."

"What happened if you broke the rules?"

"You got sent away. Like at school."

"What did you do in town? Was it a big place? Were there restaurants and cinemas?"

"There was everything I wanted. A Rabbi. He was willing to convert me."

"Wasn't it hard for you, the prohibitions, the rules you surely couldn't have believed in?"

"I was used to rules. It didn't bother me. But he was a very intelligent man. He explained to me the rules were only there to help people toward the goal."

"Which was?"

"To survive. To go on surviving as Jews."

"That meant something to you?"

"It gave me a reason to live. To survive as Rachel; I had to survive because the Jews had to survive. Because they were as they were. It was their right. It was the basic right."

"So you got converted to being a Jew?"

"I already was a Jew. I just wanted the document."

"Did you become observant? Obey all the rules and regulations?"

"I didn't have to. I had the numbers on my wrist. I told him. I said I don't know if I'll ever have a home. If I do, it won't be kosher."

"'It doesn't really matter at all.'"

"As I said, he was intelligent. He understood."

"Did you get your document?"

"Yes."

"Can I see it?"

"I tore it up."

I was shocked. The bureaucrat in me was horrified. "Why? You never tear up papers!"

"It was only for me. It wasn't for anyone else."

"Is it what makes you a Jew?"

"It is what made me not a German."

"When did you leave the Sanatorium?"

"Just over a year after I arrived. The Director sent for me. He was jovial. He told me I was cured. It didn't mean I could live like everybody else. Yet. For a year, I must not work, mustn't strain myself, no late nights, no strenuous sports; fresh air, good food. A boyfriend, yes, but, nothing serious, no sex, did I understand? No harm in a kiss or two, pretty girl, hey?"

"I asked, 'Are you sending me away?'

"'I'm sending you home, young lady. Where was that place you came from, ah! (shuffling of papers), Mauthausen, nice little village I'm sure, plenty of good air, good food, you'll be fine.'

"'Mauthausen is not a village.

"'I beg your pardon. Civic pride, very proper, very commendable. Your nice little town, then. Shall I write to your family? Your family doctor, how is he called?'

"I went back to Mauthausen. My doctor had been posted. There was a new man, a Major.

"He looked at my papers.

"'You don't belong in the hospital. You're not sick. Where do you want to go?'

"'I don't know.'

"'Shall I send you back to Leipzig?'

"'Why?'

"'Didn't you live there?' Delicately, 'Do you have family?'

"'No.'

"'No-one in Leipzig?'

"So he sent me over the fence, to Mauthausen. Symbolically, it was a terrible journey. There were the new huts, clean, with separate beds for everybody, twelve to a hut.

"They had planted flowers and bushes, it looked pleasant. The food was starchy, but plentiful. There were men around as well as women, even some children, reunited families, or, more often, bits of families. There were infants, products of some terrible optimism; or of some affirmation, like mine.

"There were concerts, organised by earnest Americans, in an outdoor cinema. People were cautiously social. They recognised each other. They spoke. They even had special friends.

"The barbed wire fences had been replaced by a neat wooden one. The gates were open. The U.S. Army sentry's gun lay at his feet. He liked to chat with the kids. There were no dogs. You could stay, or go, as you pleased.

"There was nowhere to go. It was still a Camp. My hut was not two metres from where Lisa died. Then someone took me to an 'assefa'."

"To a what?"

I had no idea she was using a Hebrew word.

"A meeting. There were people from Palestine in the Camp. They were part of Aliya Beth."

I knew, of course, all about Aliya Beth. It was part of modern history, we were taught it in Fifth grade. It meant illegal immigration of Jews without certificates, Jews who were not included in the limited quota of 'certificated immigrants' stipulated in the British White Paper. After the War, few Jews could enter Palestine legally. Rachel had had no idea of any of this.

"What did they tell you?"

"There were about fifty of us, mostly young people, but not all. There were many such 'assefot'. They couldn't talk to too many people at a time, it was all secret. One person told another.

"It was supposed to be a lecture on 'Music Appreciation'."

"He told us about Palestine. He didn't make it sound very attractive. The Arabs were fighting the Jews, the British were hanging them. There was going to be a Jewish State, but it would have to be fought for. Getting there at all was very tricky. No one would sell them decent boats nor had they the money to pay for them, if they could be found.

"They used small cargo boats, overloaded, and tried to sneak into Palestine's more deserted shores, after dark. The British patrolled the beaches, British boats patrolled the seas. If a boatload was caught, the immigrants were put into Camps, a bit like Mauthausen as it was now. But behind barbed wire fences and closed gates; in Cyprus. A prison camp.

"What would happen to them, how long would they stay there? Nobody knew.

"Worse, those of the ships that were still seaworthy were often escorted back to Europe. We could find ourselves in Mauthausen again, with this time no hope, no hope at all.

"He asked us: 'Any questions?' "

"Why are the British doing this? I thought they were on our side?"

" 'Nobody is on our side.'

"'But why this?'

"'Because there are a hundred million Arabs soaking in oil and three hundred thousand Jews with nothing. Which side would you bet on for when the time comes to return a favour for a favour?'
"'Are the British hated?'
"'Well, a bit. They're also admired. They fought Hitler for a long time, alone. We try to look on it as a family quarrel.'
"'What would happen to us?'
"'Probably most of you would go to kibbutzim. Work. Learn Hebrew. Build a Jewish State. Fight for it, too, when the time comes.'
It didn't sound like an easy life.
"'Why a Jewish State?'
"'How can you ask?'
"There were a lot more questions. They didn't matter, though. What alternative had we? And the bottom line was attractive. These people actually wanted us. Risked their lives for us. Waited for us, anxiously, on the shores.

"We were the embarrassment of Europe. There were conferences and commissions but there weren't any offers.

"We all wanted to go to Palestine. We were mad for family, to be part of a nation of our own.

"His name was Dov. They all had short names like that, Dov or Uzi or Zvi, as if there wasn't time to use longer syllables, there was just too much you had to get on with.

"He said, 'If there's anyone interested, will he please stand up?'
"Everyone stood.
"He said, 'OK. Someone will talk to each of you separately. You,' he pointed to one young man, 'make me a list of your names and what huts you are in. First names, only. Remember, as of this minute, you are illegals. You are responsible for each others' fate, maybe even lives. Don't talk. I'll be in touch. Just wait.'

"But of course, we talked. A touch of family; a touch of hope.
"It was a woman, a young woman, twenty-five, perhaps, who came to see me. Her name was Shosh. She said, 'In about a week, we'll move you out of Mauthausen.'
"'To where?'
" 'Don't know exactly. Maybe another Camp.'
"'How long will I stay there?'
"'Depends. Depends on what boats we can get, how things go. We'll put you into trucks, and on through the Alps to Italy. You'll

probably have to walk part of the way, over the border, climbing, really. One small suitcase only. You'll go at night. Through the snow.'

"I thought of my parents, who had also each packed one small case. What had they put in them - photographs, keepsakes, a lock of my hair, or just a change of clothing that they would never need?

"Shosh went on: 'Then we'll move you through Italy to the ports. You're not going to like the boat trip. There'll be hundreds of you in a boat meant to carry only a small load of cargo. You'll be in the hold. Like cargo. Too dangerous to let you stay up on deck; maybe ten minutes a day, the British ships are all over. You'll be sleeping on wooden shelves again, three to a shelf. It will be very hard.

"'If we make it, you'll be picked up at night on the shore, people from the kibbutzim, other people, in five minutes you'll be in new clothes; in half an hour you'll be sleeping innocently in your bed.

"'The British will come.'

"'Who, me? I've been here for three years, what do you mean 'illegal entry?'

"I said: 'Don't the Americans, the British, in charge of the Camps here know what you are doing?'

"'They know they house, say one thousand refugees; there are always one thousand beds filled, they don't realise the faces change. Very handy hotels, the camps. We call them by code names. This one's the Hilton. Keep it to yourself. One question: Are you healthy? As I told you, it's hard. It's a tough physical ordeal.'

"I said, 'I'm fine.'

"'No T.B? If you've tuberculosis, don't do it. We'll try to get a legal certificate.'

"'How long would that take?'

"'Truthfully, God only knows.'

"As I turned to go, she said casually, too casually: 'I'll be around here for a while. Just bring me a health certificate from a physician and a lung X-ray, will you, before I put you on the list.'

"I went straight to the new doctor at the hospital, the one I had been sent to after I was sent 'home' from the sanatorium.

"He was very jovial.

"'Of course I remember you! Doing fine? What can I do for you?'

"'Can you give me a health certificate? I mean, that I'm healthy. A clean bill of health.'

"'And what would you want that for, young lady?'

"'I have an invitation to go and live with an aunt of mine. In Australia.'

"'Well, I can't exactly do that. You know, you're not over the tuberculosis yet. You're not active, of course. But that wouldn't do for the Australians. Very strict, over there. Couldn't go around infecting their citizens could you, then there might be hospital bills, couldn't expect them to risk all that?'

"I said, 'I've nowhere else to go.'

"'Come now, young lady, it's not so bad at Mauthausen, is it? I've been over. Very cosy. Nice food. Not luxury, of course, but you can't expect luxury can you? But perfectly possible. I've heard the stories. You Jews do exaggerate, you know. Natural I suppose. Want a bit of sympathy. But you do like to moan about your troubles, blow them up to bloody nonsense.'

"I said, 'You're not American, are you?'

"'Oh dear me, no, British. On loan here. How did you know?'

"'You sounded different.

"'I'm a soldier and a doctor, just like any other. I can't give you a certificate, dear girl, but I'll give you a bit of advice. What do you want to go to Australia for? Stay here. It's your country you know, and it's in trouble, great trouble. Needs a lot of rebuilding. No time to leave the sinking ship. Why don't you get out of Mauthausen and do something for Germany, like all the other decent Germans? I know you're not too well, but you could do something light; teach, perhaps, work in an office, start with a half-day, get your country going again. Don't you think you owe that to Germany? If you Jews understood those things you might not get into half the trouble you always seem to be in. Be grateful! Do the decent thing! Don't always blame the other man. People don't like parasites you know. Look at them. In Mauthausen. Why don't these people go back to their homes and start building up their towns again? Slackers! I'm marrying a German girl, you know. Army family. Titled, too. The Right Stuff.'

"I thought of my mother. She too had perhaps belonged to an Army family, maybe titled also. But she hadn't been the 'Right Stuff'. She had fallen in love with a Jew, and married him. She had paid for it with her life.

"'Dear girl, you have to stick to your own chaps, even when they're naughty.'

"Were you angry?'
"What for? I envied him. He lived in a different world. Besides, I *was* 'sticking to my own chaps'; I was stuck to the Jews."
"I asked him curiously: 'How long have you been in Germany?'
"'Six weeks: long enough to size up people like you.'
"I went straight to one of the other doctors, one who remembered me.
"'I can't give you a certificate.'
"'Why not?'
"'I'm not your doctor. I'm a military doctor. I'm not allowed to take civilian cases. I'm sorry.'
"'What should I do?'
"'There are a couple of doctors in town you can go to. Good luck. Come back if there's anything else I can do.'
"'I will. And thank you.'
"'When you get there, send me an orange.'
"I was puzzled. 'From Australia?'
"'No, from Palestine.'"
"How did you know?"
"'Some of my best friends are Jews. Is there anything else?'
"I hesitated.
"'Out with it!'
"'I need an X-ray picture. A clean X-ray. Not mine. Some other young girl.'
"He whistled. 'You don't want much, do you? Anything else? A U.S. passport? A few gold mine share certificates?'
"'Just the X-ray. That's all.'
"'I can only give you advice. Not even that. I'm just talking to myself. Remember?'
"I nodded.
"'Have you any money? Dollars?'
"'Some.'
"'Go to the X-ray Department and ask for the technician. His name's Fred. Don't give him too much money, he's greedy. He's got a wife and six kids. You never heard this. Remember?'
"I nodded again.
"'Last chance?'
"'A windproof jacket,' I said, 'And walking boots, size 38. You can't buy them in the German shops.' I handed him a hundred dollar note.

"He waved it away. 'That would be strictly illegal. You're a civilian, you can't buy things from the Army Stores. Pick then up here tomorrow afternoon.'

I asked Rachel: "Did you send him an orange when you got to Palestine?"

"I sent him a whole box."

"Did you get the X-ray?"

"It wasn't a problem. I went up to him: 'Are you Fred?'

"'Yes.'

"'I want to talk you. Can you slip out for a few minutes?'

"He leered.

"'I fancy you alright but I've got a wife and six kids. And no money.'

"'I want to give you money.'

"'Something illegal? I can't get you any drugs. Try the pharmacist.'

"'Not drugs. Not even illegal, really. Come.'

"He took off his white coat and we went outside. I told him what I wanted. A good clean pair of lungs. My name on the film. And today's date. Typed on hospital notepaper, with the usual notation for negative results. I'd see to the signature, all I needed was the radiologist's name.

"He said, 'That's forgery.'

"'Not yours. It's just copying, really. No signature.'

"He said he would do it for one hundred dollars and I gave him half on account. He said it was a risk.

"I promised, 'No-one will see it till I get to Australia.'

"Then I went back to Mauthausen.

"The next morning, I took a train into town. I stopped a woman on the street. 'I'm looking for a doctor.' She looked me up and down. 'Don't worry dearie, it don't show. One of them Americans?' She lifted one leg and jiggled it up and down in an obscene gesture. 'Jig-jig, two hundred cigarettes, eh? I don't know any doctor like that. Only one I know is a young chap, straight from school into the army, only a couple of months in private practice, he wouldn't know much about that.'

"I asked for his address. He sounded fine to me.

"He was no problem at all. I told him I needed a health certificate for a job tutoring two girls privately in their home. I was wary of 'Australia', he might have been a German patriot for all I knew.

"He said, 'Are you healthy?'
"'I feel fine.'
"'Any childhood illnesses?'
"'Almost none. Measles, I think.'
"'T.B.?'
"'Pardon?'
"'Tuberculosis.' He was already writing 'none'.
"'Social diseases?'
"'I don't know what you mean.' I knew of course. They were a death sentence in the SS Camp.

"He gave me the certificate. He hadn't examined me at all. He didn't look at me.

"'How much?'
"'Fifty dollars.'

"He knew I was up to something. If not, it would have been much less, and in Deutschmarks.

"I paid him. He didn't say a word.

"I picked up my X-ray picture, and the note. They looked fine. I gave Fred the money I owed him. I signed the note with a scribble. I picked up my jacket and boots, there were socks, and gloves too. He had left them with his nurse.

Then I waited for Shosh.

15. ISRAEL, 1979

Avi said: "I haven't been honest with you."
"I know."
"How did you know?"
I knew because I had never reached Avi at his still centre. He had always evaded me. I had told him everything about me. I had told him about Uri, my grandmother, Rachel, I had denied him nothing of myself. He had not reciprocated. He had held back. I had thought that perhaps he was just a very private person.
"Who is she?"
"What are you talking about?"
"I presume," I said with quaking dignity, "there is another woman."
"It's not that, Gerda. You're woman enough for me. It's much more complicated. And it's worse. My real name is Ibrahim, not Avi. I'm an Arab."
I thought he was a spy. "You're not born here? You're not a Sabra? Who are you?"
"It's not that bad. Yes, I'm a Sabra, yes I was born here, it's not what you're thinking, I'm an Israeli Arab, I'm as loyal to this country as you are. For God's sake I fought for it! It's just I'm not a Jew."
"Oh Avi," I said, "that's all it is? Why didn't you tell me? You know I'm not a religious person. What the bloody hell does it matter? Did you think I'd care?"
I truly didn't. I was overcome with relief. I put my arms round him. He didn't move.
"It matters. I can't marry you. At least, not here. God knows I want to, but I don't know if you'd agree."
It was the second time he had mentioned God. "What's the problem? Are you a devout Moslem?" I suddenly realised his parents hadn't come from Romania and might not even be dead. "Will your parents object?"
Avi said with an effort. "Sit down. I'll tell you the whole story. Then you can decide what you want to do."
I didn't want to sit down. The bells were ringing in my head. There was no other woman. Everything else I was sure would be a lot of nonsense to me. But I obediently took a chair. I was desperate to know and it wasn't worth wasting time arguing. "Go ahead."

"OK." A long breath. "I'm an Arab, my real name is Ibrahim (hence Avi) Husseini. I have one brother. My parents are dead. My father was an Egyptian, my mother was born in Jaffa, we lived in Haifa. My brother studied also at the Technion in Haifa, also engineering, he got his degree summa cum laude and he couldn't get a fucking job. Except as a high school teacher. He didn't want to teach. He is a naval engineer. He wanted to build ships. Only the Navy builds ships around here. He couldn't get into the Navy because he isn't a Jew."

"So what did he do?"

"He became a high school teacher of course. Very fed up."

"Is he bitter?"

"Not bitter. It's understandable. Just bloody fed up. I didn't want to be like that. So when I was seventeen I became Avi, a Jewish kid."

"Did you convert?"

"Hell, no. I wouldn't be able to go through a religious conversion. I just got false papers."

"How does one do that?"

"No problem. There's a fellow in Ramle. Specialist. Anything you like. Works mostly for the PLO. Israeli identity card, a hundred dollars, come back tomorrow."

I was a bit shocked.

"I wasn't out to become a criminal, Gerda. I just wanted a normal chance. I didn't mind serving in the Army. I love this country. I owe it. I don't care who the enemy is, Arabs or Christian Scientists or Hottentots, I'm ready to defend this place. But I did want a job. A real job, not stagnation in some backward village. Gerda, I'm a research man. I want to achieve something in my work. I want to know, to understand, to develop, I want to be known as the robotics fellow, I want to make changes in how things are done. I'm an ambitious man, I admit it."

I said, "Avi, I can understand all that. I just don't see how it affects us. You're an Israeli. I'm an Israeli. What do I care if you're an Arab? You've got a job, you're doing research, you're happy in your work. Why can't we get married? In Cyprus, a civil marriage if you like?"

"I wish it was that easy. I thought it might be like that. It isn't. I have to leave the lab. I can't go on."

I was puzzled. Only a few weeks ago, Avi and I had been invited to dinner with his boss. Nice guy. Said how impressed he was with Avi's research. The research side was going to be expanded, Avi would be promoted; there were big things ahead. I had been so pleased. Avi liked him, too. I reminded him.

"That's the problem. The emphasis on the research is because we've landed a Defence contract. On the basis of some work I did.

"Very hush-hush. Top secret. My papers got me into the army, into my job, they'll never pass a real high-class security check... the kind you need for top secret. Mossad, poking among the neighbours; 'How long have you known this man?' One look at my ID card under the microscope, I'd be in jail before you could look around."

"You haven't committed a crime."

"Oh yes, I have, my dear. Concealment of identity. False papers. False declarations. I might get away with a scolding in the present circumstances, but if I were involved in a top security job, very suspicious indeed.

"Very nasty grilling, probably a few years in jail, and someone following me for the rest of my life. I've always anticipated something like this. That's why I've never let myself get in deep with a woman. I've always got out in time. Until now."

I said, "What are you going to do?"

"Gerda, I'm going to leave. As a matter of fact, I've already handed in my resignation. This is my country, it hurts like hell to leave it. It burns in me, but there's nothing else I can do. I'm fairly well-known already. I've got an offer of a very good job. Come with me! We can get married anywhere you like. I love you very much, I love the idea of a child. Does it matter so much where we make our home?"

"Where's the job?"

"In Germany."

Later, when we were in bed, Avi began to make love to me. He put his arms round me and kissed my mouth. How acute he was, how sensitised.

"You don't want to, do you?"

"Of course I do."

"Don't lie. Never fake it with me."

I didn't want to make love. I wasn't sure I wanted him to touch me at all. This worried me.

He said, "Don't be upset. It's natural enough. We have to talk." So we talked. After a bit, he put his arm round me again, and it was alright. Or almost alright.

"Why Germany? Couldn't it be anywhere else?"

"I wrote to a dozen places. The only one to come up with a definite offer was this firm in Germany."

"Couldn't you try a few more?"

"It wouldn't work. The guy in Munich knows me. At least, he knows my father. He worked with him. He knows who I am."

"Where did he work with your father? Was your father an engineer too?"

"No, he was administrative officer of a large engineering project. In Egypt."

"War project?"

"Yes, it was a war project. World War II. Gerda, that war's long over, it's been forty years."

I wasn't so sure it *was* over. "What's the name of the firm?"

"Hoechtbender. Big industrial giant, has a dozen plants, different products."

"Armaments, too?"

"Yes, armaments too. Among other things. But I'm an R&D man. Just robotics. I don't make the tanks."

"Do they sell to the Arab countries?"

"Gerda, I just don't know. Truthfully, I guess they do. Who doesn't? This is the only place I can go."

"Because of your papers?"

"Yes, because of my papers. Any work I do is bound to be classified. The Germans aren't slobs, they'll know. This is the only place that will take me, as I am. Never in America. Not even in Britain and France. They wouldn't know what side I am on. They wouldn't want an Arab with a false identity in their most sensitive security labs."

"And the Germans do?"

"The Vice-President of this particular firm was my father's friend. He's willing to take a chance on me. He understands. They've offered me a five-year contract. With a house. Repayments of course, but over five years, no problem. I told them I was getting married. It was the first thing I thought of. Gerda, marry me! You won't regret it. It's in Munich, a nice town. I get my own laboratory and pretty much a free hand. After five years, if I do a decent job, I can probably take my choice of where to go. We might even be able to come back."

We'd never be able to come back. Hoechtbender. Shin Bet would go over him with a microscope if he ever tried to enter Israel again. Five years of repayments. They knew how to pin him down. Tactfully.

I said miserably. "I want to marry you. I don't know if I can live in Germany. Especially not in Munich. Where it all began."

"Why not? They're not the same people. The people you're thinking about are all old people, or dead. The new generation is different. They're tolerant, liberal, pro-Israel. They're ashamed of the past. How can you hold them responsible - they weren't even born at the time!"

I didn't know how to explain it to him. On my wrist was tattooed an invisible number. I saw it, Rachel saw it. Avi did not.

"I don't know," I said. "Let me think about it. I'll try."

Of course I went to Rachel. I told her everything.
"You knew he was an Arab?"
"I thought he might be."
"How did you know?"
"Oh, the way he moved, spoke. Remember, I lived among them most of my life." That explained the familiarity I had sensed between them, when she had come to dinner at our flat.
"Could you live in Germany?" I asked.
"No."
Of course not. She wouldn't even get into my German car.
"Why not? They're a new generation. It wasn't their fault."
I was quoting Avi.
"There isn't any rational reason. It's like being a claustrophobe. Not being able to go into a small room or an elevator or a plane."

I said, "Like eating pork for a religious Jew? A sin, a violation. Contamination. You'd rather die?"
She nodded.
"Help me, Rachel," I pleaded. "Tell me what to do. I love him."
"What do I know about love?" she said.

16. THE ROAD TO PALESTINE, 1947

Nothing happened for a week. Then Shosh came. All bustle.
"Pack your suitcase! We're off in half a hour."
"Where to?"
"Down the line. Very good 'hotel', the Savoy. Only a couple of nights though, then over the border. Do you have warm clothes, good walking shoes? If not, I'll get you some. We supply everything. No honest request refused. Do you need sanitary towels?"
I said: "No."
"Let's see your medical reports and the X-ray." She had a memory like a fox.
I gave her the documents. She read the report and snorted. "You're ready for the Olympics, according to this." She looked at the X-ray report. She said, "It's forged."
"How do you know?"
"I don't know. I just have a smell for it. I've seen so many of them. Dozens, every day. I've watched it done. We have a very good Forgery Department. Immigration Certificates. We manufacture dozens every week. Passports, too."
She wasn't looking at me. Finally, she did.
"I can't take you," she said. "I knew it. I know T. B. when I see it. You wouldn't make it, kid. You wouldn't make it marching over the Alps. You'd be spitting blood."
"Let me try," I said. "Please."
"I'd be a murderer if I did. You'll have to wait."
"How long?" How long was it since I had wept?
"Not long. Just give me a couple of weeks. You won't have to wait for a certificate. We'll take you as an illegal by the carriage trade."
"What way is that?"
"By train to Italy."
"I haven't got a passport. I haven't got any papers at all."
"You will baby, you will. Leave it to Mama Shosh. Two weeks. Not more!"
She was back in two minutes.
"Did you say you had warm clothes?"
"Yes. Boots too. And gloves."

"Would you mind if I took them? For another one of our clients. You won't need them, you know. Not the way you'll go."

"You're welcome."

She took out the clothes and looked at them. Brand new. Everything was still marked 'PX'.

"You've got some fine friends," she said. "Very upper class."

"Another thing: do you have a photograph? Just your head and shoulders. Front view."

"I have one on the *laisser-passer* the hospital got me to enter Switzerland. Would that do?"

"Fetch it, luv. It will do just fine."

Two weeks she said. And this time, she really went.

She didn't come back for fifteen days. I was angry.

"You're a day late."

"Marked them off, did you? That's nice. I'm truly sorry. Air strike at Heathrow. Anyway, here I am."

She sat down on my bed. She looked awful - grey face, red-rimmed eyes. She interpreted my look.

"Nothing's wrong. I'm just tired. One good night's sleep..." She opened her suitcase. It was neatly packed with a variety of clothing. Underwear, dresses, sweaters and skirts - and the uniform of a Red Cross Nurse. She took out a British passport and handed it to me. I flipped it open. It belonged to one Elaine Greenberg, aged eighteen, born in Ealing, London. But it was my picture that stared back at me.

"It looks terrific." I had never seen a British passport before, but it seemed real to me.

She handed me another. Susan Greenberg, age twenty-six, born ditto.

I said, "Hey, that's you!"

"They're real, you know, apart from the little matter of your photograph. Susan Greenberg, that's me. Elaine's my little sister."

"Have you done this before?"

"We do 'borrow' rather a lot of passports. Only from reliable people, of course. It's a trickle, we get in a few hundred that way. But all off-quota. Every person counts."

The idea that I 'counted' was a new one for me. I put it aside for the moment.

"We're doing it luxury all the way. Local train to Munich, Express to Rome. After that, we'll see. There won't be any trouble at the border, the Italians don't much care."

I said, "I'm supposed to be British. I don't speak English at all."
"I know. You're just not going to talk. Big scarf" - she drew it out. It was big all right - woollen and at least two metres long. "Tooth operation; we'll pad your mouth with cotton wool. Taking my little sister for treatment, botched up job in Austria, letter to prove it."
"Why Rome?"
"I live there. I really do. It's convenient. Any more questions?"
"A million. But I can't think of them now. When do we leave?"
"Tomorrow. I have to have a night's sleep. Is there a spare bed in the barracks?"
"Several." Only yesterday our population had experienced one of its no longer mysterious downs.

I pointed out a vacant bunk and she climbed into it. "Now I'll show you my party trick." She closed her eyes and was instantly asleep.

In the morning a Red Cross Nurse, trim in a clean uniform, shook my shoulder. "Let's get some breakfast, and be off."

Nothing went wrong on the way to Rome, except that the trains were crowded and we couldn't talk. I practised some convincing noises and inaudible whispers consisting of nonsense words. I got a great deal of sympathy. I also got very hungry and even more thirsty. The cotton pad bulged my cheek convincingly but it also dried my mouth.

After a couple of hours, Shosh said, "It's time I changed your dressing." and unpacked a bulky First Aid kit. We went to the lavatory and squeezed in together and she opened the kit and took out the cotton wool and gave me a bottle of water and some bread and sausage.

After that, she packed in more cotton wool. We were nearing the frontier. She put in a lot, so much that I really could only whisper inaudibly and say, "G-ga-ga."

"Splendid. We'll change your dressing again in a couple of hours."

The man who came on to the train for passport control was very sympathetic. "How do you feel?"

"Ga," I said.

I was very tired when we got to Rome. Shosh looked at me.

"You can't imagine how much worse it would have been, going over the mountains. It can take days, weeks, even. Waiting for patrols. Waiting for the time of least activity. Small groups. Waiting again until the one before is safely across. Always at night. Freezing temperatures, no hot food or drink."

"What about the trucks?"

"Oh, they're our Austrian fleet. They have to turn back ten miles before the border. We can't cross openly, you know. No-one has any papers. The Italian trucks wait for us ten miles across on the other side."

At Rome we took a taxi to the flat. It was quite big: five rooms, all of them empty, except for beds, and lots of clothing, men and women's, flung all over the place.

"Who lives here?"

"Oh, this one and that. Not all at the same time, fortunately."

"Where do you live in Israel?"

"Kibbutz. In the north."

"Are you married?"

"In a way. Meaning, yes, I'm married, but we haven't lived together much."

"Where is he? At the kibbutz?"

"Actually, no. He's here. I was hoping he'd be at the flat. We're in the same business. We get a couple of days, a few hours together, every now and then."

"Do you miss not being with him all the time?"

"I suppose. But we do get some time together. It's the kids I miss."

"You have children?"

"We've got a boy and a girl...five and three years old. They hardly know me. They call me 'auntie'. They hug me and kiss me, they're very affectionate, then they run back to their kindergarten mother. Her, they call 'Mum'."

"Oh Shosh!"

"I know. You never get the time back. Shut up, will you? Take a shower. Raid the fridge, or go to sleep. I have to make a call."

She was on the phone a long time. Then she came into the kitchen. I was eating a sandwich. I made her one, too. There was good Italian bread, and cheese.

She said, "I'm afraid it's the end of the line. Give me the passport. They're on to us."

She took her passport and mine and cut them into little pieces, then put them in an ashtray and set them alight. They burned well.

"What will we do now?"

"Well, we part. I'm going back to Germany. I'm afraid you're going to have to get to Palestine with the ordinary illegals. By boat."

"How will you get back, without a passport?"

"Oh, I hardly ever need it. We have our ways."

"What happens to me?"

"You'll be picked up when a ship's ready. It isn't going to be a picnic. I'm sorry."

"Don't worry," I said. I was rather pleased. It would be an adventure. "I'll be just fine."

She kissed me. "My husband's coming. And I'll be off early. I probably won't see you again. Until you come and visit me in Palestine. If I'm there. The fridge is full, there's a money box on the mantelpiece. Don't go out more than you have to. Our people could come for you at any time.

"I nearly forgot. Don't open the door unless they give you the password," she said. "It's an English expression, from the theatre. It means good luck. Write it down, you mustn't forget. Here, I'll write it for you."

She handed me the piece of paper. "Say it."

I said, in German accented English, "Break a leg!"

In the morning, the flat was empty. I stayed there, alone, for four days.

I used the money sparingly. There wasn't much food in the shops, anyway. I was quite happy with bread and cheese. I bought myself a pair of socks, a sweater, and two pairs of knickers. I bought a book 'Teach yourself English' but gave it back when I realised it was in Italian. There were only Hebrew and English books in the flat.

A man turned up. He gave the password, and I let him in. He was friendly, but taciturn. He had a shower and a meal, then he went away again.

Two days after that first visitor there was a knock at the door, a man's voice gave me the password, so I opened it. Before me stood two British officers.

I went white and tried to shut the door.

They laughed in my face and pushed their way in.

"Calm down," the Captain said, in perfect German. "We're not the British Army. We're Aliya Beth."

He introduced me to 'Colonel Mackintosh' ('one of the lads'; later to become quite prominent in the Mossad.).

"We've got a jeep outside," he said. "Can you be ready in ten minutes?" I was ready in five.

We drove out of Rome. The signposts indicated Livorno. We took that road. We drove for two hours. There was an Italian army checkpoint. They waved their conquerors on, with a bow.

We stopped two hours later, at a place where there was nothing at all. We were surrounded by a small forest.

The jeep drew up just off the road behind a clump of trees. We walked down a broad path. It had wheel marks on it.

A few minutes later, we came to a clearing. In it were army trucks, empty. About three hundred people, some of them, mainly the children, were paddling in a stream that ran through. They looked exhausted. They were talking to each other. They spoke German, Yiddish, some Polish, a little Russian. Hungarian, too.

They were my people.

After a while, we piled into the trucks. There were narrow benches, very close together. The tarpaulins were closed, it was hard to breathe.

"Sorry," said the Colonel. "And remember, no talking. None at all. We don't know how many road-blocks we have to pass yet. If we stop, don't even breathe."

We travelled in convoy, the jeep at the front. There were road blocks, many stops. We held our breath. We travelled for hours. Towards the end, I began to cough. People moved up and they put me near the back, where there was a little more air.

Then we stopped. For a long time. An hour or two, maybe. I thought I'd die.

Finally, they opened the tarpaulin. We got out. They passed round paper cups of water, and biscuits. We moved on stiff limbs. The children cried. Colonel Mackintosh came up to where I was sitting, with some others, on a low stone wall. We were in a port. The sea was in front of us. He pointed.

"There's your ship," he said.

It wasn't a ship. It was tiny. It looked more like a rowing boat. It was dirty, and rode the water heavily.

"That?" someone asked him. "For all of us?"

"Everyone," he said.

Somehow we all got on board. We stood on the deck. We were close enough to be touching, but there was a fresh breeze. I thought it might not be so bad.

A kid who looked about seventeen (actually, he was twenty-one) raised a megaphone.

"This is your Captain speaking!" He spoke in Hebrew. One of us - he was an ex-cantor, the religion had gone, but he still had his Hebrew - translated for him into German in a loud, stentorian cantor's voice.

Other people in the crowd of us on deck were translating simultaneously to each other in any of the half a dozen languages required.

"This ship carries a Portuguese flag and its name - you see it painted on the front - is 'Fiore'. Out of Lisbon. We are carrying sheets of asbestos to Piraeus.

"In reality, this is a Jewish ship. You are the asbestos. Our name is 'Atideinu', which means 'Our Future'.

"When we reach the territorial waters of Palestine, we will haul down our flag of convenience and raise our Jewish flag. On this occasion, we will salute the flag and sing 'Hatikvah'. If you don't know our national anthem, start learning it now.

"I am God on this ship, like any other Captain. I will be obeyed. If there is a doctor on board, will you raise your hand?" Five hands went up. "You are, as of now, the Passengers' Committee. You are not kapos. You will not enforce any rules. All rules must be democratically agreed on. But you will bring me all passengers' complaints and requests every day at nine a.m. I will talk only to you. You understand why. I have to sail this ship. It is not an easy ship to sail.

"You will have seen that this is not the Ritz. You will all have to remain at all times below, except for ten minutes, each person, once a day, In groups of no more than four.

"You must understand that British frigates are patrolling these waters. They are very suspicious of ships like ours. That is why we carry asbestos - it is not a healthy material. We hope they will not look.

"Are there any pregnant women on board?" Again, five hands. "Anyone near term?"

One. "Do not worry, madam, you have five physicians. We will clear a space on deck. But will you please try to have it at night? It will be safer for all of us."

He may have looked seventeen but he had all the self-confidence and command of a man who was fully mature.

"We will be sailing in one hour. At that time, you will all go below. I wish you a pleasant voyage. Any questions?"

A doubtful, "Excuse me, Sir, but have you sailed a boat like this before?"

"Nobody has sailed a boat like this before. In fact, I was the only candidate in the world for the post of Captain of this ship." He leaned on the rail theatrically. It promptly gave an ominous cracking. He grinned. "Don't worry. I'll get you there."

"Anything else?"

"Why aren't there any lifeboats?"

"Because we can't. A freighter with a five-man crew can't have the half a dozen lifeboats that you'd need on deck for three hundred persons. It's just a chance we have to take. Anyone who wants to leave can do so right now."

No-one left. In precisely one hour, the motor sounded, and we went below. We were elated and cheerful.

It was far worse than I had ever imagined. It was the Mauthausen Death Camp again, with its triple wooden shelves. It smelt already, maybe from the last lot, and it would smell for ever more. In addition to the usual excretions, there would be a lot of sea-sickness; the tiny vessel rolled like a tub.

The hatches were open. Nobody crowded them. It wasn't like Mauthausen at all. The elation did not leave us. Everyone was immensely kind to each other, aware of each other, polite.

'Am I in your way?'

'Not at all.'

The physicians went round. They had been given blue armbands. They listened sympathetically and made notes. They had childrens' copybooks, and pens.

The smell became indescribable. On the second day, we asked for a sanitation squad. Pots got emptied faster, and it was better, but not much. On the fourth day, I began to cough again. One of the doctors came up to me.

"Are you alright?"

"It's nothing. Just a cold. I caught a chill in Rome."

"There's blood on your handkerchief."

"I cut my hand."

"Look here, I'm going to get you outside for an extra half hour, if the Captain agrees."

The idea terrified me. "The others won't stand for it."

"It isn't a Camp, you know. These are people. Your fellow Jews." He came back the same day. He said, "Come."

He took me on deck. He led me to the stern of the ship. There was a big pile of ropes. "Behind there."

"Half an hour?"

"All day. The Captain's suggestion. If it's warm enough, at night too."

"Was he thinking of me, or the other passengers?"

"Both. Just keep your head down."

I couldn't have had better attention. Doctors visited me two or three times a day. I couldn't help laughing. They were all mature men, but they crawled over to me on their hands and knees. Discipline was strict.

It was quiet. It was beautiful. A Mediterranean cruise. I was still spitting blood.

The Captain and the Engineer had a smoke together, standing quite near me, leaning cautiously on the rail. They had probably forgotten about me. One of the doctors was with me. He made a sign to me to be quiet. They were talking in English. He wanted to hear.

"How's the engine doing?"

"Like my grandmother. Every stroke I think it's her last."

"I thought you had it overhauled in Brindisi?"

"She doesn't need an overhaul, she needs a grave. RIP. She must be about ninety years old."

"Tell her she has to die in the Holy Land. Moshe's got his problems too. She leaks like a sieve, he's pumping twenty-four hours a day. He swears the pump could make him a fortune at any antique auction, he thinks it could be the first one ever constructed."

"Passengers OK?"

"Poor buggers. They think we've only got to get them there, after that it'll all be Paradise."

"How's Lotte?"

"Fine, as far as I know. She's pregnant. Swears it's mine, though I can't think when."

"Your first?"

"No, our twelfth. Sorry, I meant it's the twelfth for our kibbutz, Hanita. It's the first for Lotte and me."

"What did they say?" I asked the doctor.

He told me.

We were at sea for ten days. Twice, we were spotted by a British navy ship. Each time, the Captain took over the megaphone. He spoke a mixture of English and rough garble which I suppose he hoped sounded like Portuguese. "You wanna come aboard?"

"Hey. You welcome! Garble, garble, garble. You got any whiskey? Garble, ASBESTOS, we goin' Piraeus, Greek girls very nice, garble. We gotta couple aboard, you wanna try 'em? Very clean, very lovin'. They no give you clap, hell, maybe a leetle, wassamatter, every man got clap, you no tell your wife! You like boys, eh? We got boys."

They let him go.

Each time, he warned us, in a whisper: "This is your Captain speaking. There are British ships in the vicinity. No-one, I repeat no-one goes on deck till I say so. No talking. I'm going to tack around a bit, drunken Captain looking for Piraeus, don't move, hold on to something or lie on your bunks."

Every day, precisely at noon, he gave us our position and made any announcements. It was as if we were on a proper ship.

On the tenth day, in the evening, as it was just getting chilly, I huddled under my blanket, unexpectedly the megaphone went live.

"We are just entering Palestinian territorial waters. We are going to heave to and put up the flag. You may not see it, but you will all stand and sing Hatikvah or any bits of it you've learned."

I saw the flag go up. Blue and white, with the Star of David. I heard them sing. Some knew the words, some didn't, few knew what they meant. The ex-cantor roared them out and the others followed. The Captain and the crew were singing too. So did I. There were enough tears to sink the boat.

"Poor buggers." I too, remembered those who had perished. But I was in euphoria, like all the rest. I had forgotten I was going to die of tuberculosis. I was going to begin my life at last!

17. PALESTINE, 1947

The landing went like a military operation. We anchored in three feet of water. Whispers were passed on. "Just go down the plank. Wade to the shore."

I waded toward the shore. I wasn't there yet, when a man in the water grabbed me. I opened my mouth to scream. He said very quickly, in German, "Still. Bitte."

He carried me up the shore to a small van. There were other people from the boat there too, tearing off their wet clothes and selecting dry ones from a pile on the tail-board. I saw that the man who had carried me was only a boy, maybe sixteen, in Scouts uniform.

It took about two minutes, then about a dozen of us were all in the back of the van. The same thing was happening to the others all along the beach. The motor started up.

Suddenly, there were searchlights over the beach. "Everybody halt or we will shoot! This is the British Army."

But there was no-one there. The beach was deserted. We were all on the road. I could see the ship, there was a full moon. 'Atideinu' was painted on a panel fixed precariously to her side.

Ironically enough, our van took us to what had once been a TB sanatorium. It was a collection of crumbling concrete buildings, half in ruins, a private clinic now for asthmatics. They put me into a bed. "The British may come," they warned. "Keep your eyes closed. Don't speak."

They did. "Are you off the ship?" I didn't answer. A mild voice said, "Can't you see this poor girl is sick? You are disturbing my patients."

This was my first encounter with Dr Bar Zait. Formerly Dr Bergmann. Not any more.

The soldiers looked ashamed. Most of them didn't like the job at all. They were cheerful, decent lads. They didn't mind a fight, but not with women, that went against the grain.

I was in a room with four iron hospital beds. It was a bit rough and primitive. Bare concrete walls. There was a flush toilet and a basin, behind a screen.

One by one, the others dropped off to sleep. My cough disturbed me. Dr Bar Zait must have heard me. He appeared, with a glass of hot milk sweetened with honey.

I drank it and felt better. He took my pulse.

"What time is it?"

"After midnight. Don't talk. I'll stay with you till you fall asleep."

When I woke up in the morning, the others had gone. His wife came, with a breakfast tray. Everything was in meticulous order. Boiled egg, toast, coffee. A folded napkin. Like at home.

I looked at her. She was just like my mother. Sweet, pretty, cultured, kind. A useless woman, made for petting and little expensive treats.

I didn't ask her anything. I said "good morning" and ate. I was bursting with curiosity about this new country, this new people, what was going to happen to me. I knew I couldn't find out from her. She was still in Frankfurt or Hamburg or Cologne or wherever it had been. Passing round the cups at little, elegant teas.

Dr Bar Zait came in later. Now, in daylight, I could see that he was a man probably in his late forties, with intelligent blue eyes and the slightly maniacal restlessness of the true pioneer.

He took my temperature, and then, shockingly, laid his head on my chest. Of course he was only listening to my breathing. He didn't have a stethoscope. He probably didn't need one. Where TB was concerned, he knew all there was to know.

"Where are the others?"

"They went off early. They'll be in kibbutzim."

"Why not me?"

"Dear girl - what is your name? - Rachel? 'Our Mother', how beautiful, - dear Rachel, you are ill."

"Am I going to stay here?"

"A few days only. Alas, this is no longer a sanatorium. It was not possible, I don't have the staff. I treat asthma cases. The climate is very good for them. And they need very little nursing."

"What will happen to me?" I thought they might send me back.

He looked surprised. "We will send you to a sanatorium, of course."

During the following week, I stayed there. He wouldn't let me get out of bed. He wouldn't let me talk. But he spent quite a bit of time with me, and told me the story of his sanatorium.

He had left Germany, Dusseldorf, wisely, in 1934, with his new bride. Even without the Nazis, he was mad to settle in Palestine.

He was already a TB specialist, and had made quite a name for himself. He was attached to the city hospital. He wanted to set up a sanatorium in Palestine. He would be the physician, his wife would act as matron. His wife had smiled her pretty smile and agreed to everything he said.

His father died. He took his inheritance and bought beds and all the furnishings and equipment he thought a small sanatorium might need, even a murderous second-hand x-ray machine that spilt more radiation than it delivered. He showed me it. Painted in hospital white, it must have been one of the first ever made.

He brought all this stuff by ship to Palestine, paying, without argument, nearly the last of his money, some customs man's pipe-dream, deposited his wife in a Tel Aviv hotel, and began to look for the right place. He found it in Gedera, an old settlement, a village some twenty-five miles south of Tel Aviv. There was a wooded area to be bought practically for the asking in those days, the climate was ideal, much less humid than that of Tel Aviv, you could smell the healthy openness of the desert, only a little farther south.

Best of all, there were plenty of lunatics like he was, who saw nothing particularly difficult in building a sanatorium with their own hands.

Dr Bar Zait bought stones and cement, borrowed mixers and tools, a wheelbarrow, and they set to it. In the evenings, of course, after their real day's work was over.

The doctor worked all day, singing German lieder. He loved to build, even more than practising medicine - to work with his hands.

They did not build foundations, because they did not know about foundations. And because they did not know how, they did not build straight, or strong, or sure.

They built single room structures, realising they could not tackle anything more ambitious. About fifteen of them, among the trees. They were already crumbling before they were even finished.

The windows had no glass, because fresh air is good for tuberculosis and, besides, money was running out. But these incipient ruins were elegantly shaped, because Dr Bar Zait, who designed them, was an elegant man.

Most of them had no plumbing. When it became obvious sinks and toilets were needed, they were added, strictly on a what was most practical basis. In one building, the toilet sat, like a throne, in the middle of the room. This was for patients who found it hard to walk.

Dr Bar Zait then built a home for himself and his wife. It was ambitious, with a musicians' gallery, but it was crumbling too. In time, it was supplied with various additions, rooms for patients he wanted to supervise closely, and so on. It became a planner's nightmare.

It worked. TB patients came, and many got well, almost, it seemed, by the force of Dr Bar Zait's personality alone. Conditions were not ideal, but he simply would not let them die. He watched them night and day; he was always there. He solved all problems, with simplicity; if this one had no income, he took from another. People with too many clothes soon found themselves with less, while penniless girls acquired new night-gowns or good shoes.

The five radios were cycled among the 'wards'. The loud one provided open-air concerts. Dr Bar Zait did his endless rounds, not with a stethoscope, but with a pail of cement, some tiles and a trowel, to mend a cracking wall, a leaky roof.

Mrs Bar Zait performed woefully as matron. She was mostly in tears. In the end, he let her off, and she sat contentedly in her garden, with her knitting and her three cats. He did the nursing, too.

It only lasted till the 1940's. The country was becoming less anarchic. A medical bigwig came down from Tel Aviv and screamed murder. Dr Bar Zait, who did not concern himself with such things, was told to get a licence to run the sanatorium, then told they wouldn't give him one. The patients dispersed, sadly, each to his fate.

The sanatorium buildings were rented out to asthmatics. Dr Bar Zait changed his speciality. Asthmatics did not need much nursing care, the problem of matron and nursing staff was resolved. Some came from their two week holidays, some stayed for months or over the winter; and some for years.

Dr Bar Zait visited them, and cared for them tirelessly, as he had done for the TB cases. Again, they all lived on each other. Well-to-do (comparatively) patients employed less ill patients as cleaners or companions. The doctor arranged everything. He charged no fees.

It was a principle of his. Healing must be a gift. He lived on the rentals for the slowly dissolving ruins. He did not charge much, (his scale of charges was based on pure Marxism) but then he did not need much. He lived an inexpensive life. The people of Gedera cherished him. In this farming community, whenever fruit was picked, or vegetables gathered, a child was sent with a basketful to the Bar Zait's. When chickens were slaughtered and cooked, half a potful was sent up to his home. A roast, a stew, anything cooked, was delivered still piping hot, for it was known that Mrs Bar Zait did not know how to cook; she tried, but her efforts almost invariably ended in something quite inedible. Her husband loyally praised these burnt offerings, but he did not eat them.

Grateful patients, not permitted to pay, often gave him gifts. These stayed only briefly in the 'big house', and then were passed on to needy patients - radios, quilts, fine linen, hand-sewn sheets, treasures of the past, clocks, whatever.

There were stories. Once, Mrs Bar Zait decided she was going to try and bake a cake. By the time she got home with the eggs, the sugar and the flour, her oven was gone - 'That poor lady from Haifa has nothing to cook on!' The doctor's wife was also well-loved. Everyone realised it was hard to live with a saint.

The asthmatic patients, too, got well, perhaps out of fear of displeasing him. He and Gedera became quite well-known. He lobbied endlessly for the building of a proper sanatorium. It was the air, he said, the dry allergen-free Gedera air. They built a Geriatric Hospital, instead.

I fretted under Dr Bar Zait's care, patient, skilled and soothing as it was. I wanted to get on with my life, sanatorium if I had to, get it over. Then I would join a kibbutz. For the first time, I didn't think at all of dying, I knew I had a life to get on with.

18. ISRAEL, 1979

After Avi's revelations, we continued to live together in form, but not in content. Avi worked late at the laboratory almost every evening, and on weekends too. This went on for several weeks. Avi's boss had been upset at his intention to leave and had invited us both to dinner.

"I'd like to try to get you to change your mind. This whole new program we're going into depends on you."

"I'm sorry, Shlomo. I just can't."

"If it's money, we're prepared to go a long way."

"Thanks. But it isn't money. It's just - I need to broaden my experience. Work in a big lab where I can learn. It's a sort of long-delayed sabbatical. I really need it."

"Have it your own way, Avi. But remember we'll always take you back. Do you have a place fixed up?"

"Not definitely."

But it was definite, alright. The letters were going back and forth with astonishing frequency. Like they were lovers, I thought. This was a bit theatrical, but I was entitled.

We didn't make love. He got home late, he or I was always too tired, or maybe it wasn't good for the baby. I think he was as miserable as I was, as lost, as frightened, but he didn't let it show.

One evening, when, for a change, he was home, I said suddenly, "Avi, I want something."

"If this is a pregnant fancy I've already put a jar of pickled cucumbers in the refrigerator."

"Not pickled cucumbers. I want you to take me to a movie."

"That's easy. I was afraid it was going to be jellied pig's foot. What kind of movie do you want to see?"

"A comedy. Something funny," I said. He took me to Hadar Cinema, where they were showing "Monty Python and the Holy Grail". We came out still laughing, and holding hands. It was a golden evening, warm, soft and dark. Tel Aviv, literally, 'hill of spring'.

By the time we got home, we still hadn't spoken. Avi managed to open the door without letting go of my hand.

We went to bed and made love, quietly, and with tenderness, love that was more complete and sweeter than ever before.

After that we talked, half the night, calmly, we made plans together, at last, with a unity and honesty we had never known. There had been a test; and we had been brought together, not sundered, torn apart.

Avi had just got an invitation - he had meant to tell me - to present a paper at a Conference Hoechtbender's was sponsoring in Munich in six weeks' time. The idea was that during the Meeting, he would talk to the people at Hoechtbender's, set up the terms of his contract, and then just stay on. They generously enclosed a ticket, (one-way), a paid-up hotel reservation and a cheque for "incidental expenses". Once the contract was signed, they would cover his "moving expenses" too. It was a generous offer.

We decided that we would go together. There was an "accompanying persons" programme, trips and visits to castles and museums, and the countryside, or I could just wander around. This would be a sort of a "trial marriage" - to Germany, not to Avi. I was married to Avi already, with all my heart and soul. Afterwards, we would get legally married and even have a honeymoon before Avi got set into work.

"The Moselle valley," suggested Avi. "We could rent a car. They might even buy me a car, you never know. Pretty little villages. Sampling the wines."

"Not the Moselle," I said swiftly. "Couldn't we be married in Paris? And then take a trip down the Loire valley? Chambord, Blois, Amboise?"

"Certainly," said Avi swiftly, "Why not?"

It wasn't even a fissure. Just a hairline crack. Nothing to it. If you were careful.

I would also resign my job. I didn't much like it anyway. In fact, except for Dr Lustig, I hated it. So that was alright. But I wouldn't yet sell my apartment. I wouldn't sell my car.

"Let me have them as an insurance policy," I pleaded. "I told you, I'm going to give it a try. I just don't want to burn my boats."

They had sent him naturalisation papers. It was part of the deal, because of the security aspects. We made light of it. "Naturalisation," I said, "sounds like organic farming." We both laughed. Was my laughter malicious? Was I thinking of the horse droppings my father used to shovel up from the street for garden manure every time a horse and cart went by, when I was a child, in Jerusalem?

I wasn't going to be "naturalised". But when Avi wrote to them he was engaged to be married (again, this made us both laugh - it was so passé), they sent him an air ticket for me too, and booked a double room. Not so old-fashioned, after all.

"Why aren't you sure, Gerda? Is it because I am an Arab?" How could I explain to him? Being an Arab didn't matter at all. Being a German did.

"I don't know if I can live there. It's nothing to do with you."

"Does it matter so much where we live? Is it so important?"

Anywhere else wouldn't have been. I looked at the invisible numbers on my wrist. They were part of me.

I went to see Dr Lustig, and handed him my resignation, all nicely written out.

"What's all this?" he said.

"I'm getting married."

"So?"

"I can't go on working here. We're going to live abroad."

"Where?"

"Germany."

"Why?"

"It's complicated." But he was my father. I told him everything. Including all my reservations and doubts.

He said, "I'll put you on indefinite leave."

This was not reassuring. I needed bolstering up, not confirmation of my fears.

"No thanks. I'm resigning." I said firmly. There were always other jobs.

Dr Lustig got up, moved ponderously around his desk. "I hope you'll be very happy," he said, and shook my hand.

Then he grabbed me to him and squeezed me firmly, the buttons on his jacket leaving marks on my face. "Be happy, my dear. I do so hope you'll be happy." There were tears in his eyes.

"It's a boy, you know, I did an ultrasound yesterday. They said it's absolutely clear, he's a monster. I'm going to name him after you."

"No, don't do that, Gerda."

"Why not? What is your first name, anyway?" He had always been just Dr Lustig to me.

"I've got three, Wolfgang Herman Klaus. Call him something else," he said.

The other person I wanted to say goodbye to at the time was Evelyn. I delayed it to the last possible moment, because I knew she would make me feel uncomfortable. I was fond of Evelyn, for good reasons. She was giving, she was on my side, she was liberal, free-thinking, understanding, unshakeable and kind. In short, she was a bit too much. I didn't want a perfect friend, I needed an imperfect, stupid loving mother, an impregnable, hard and prejudiced rock that I could lean on and battle against. Ungrateful.

I told her bluntly, hoping to arouse just a mite of apprehension. She went straight for the bull's eye.

"Do you love him?"

"I love him to bits."

"Then, go for it," said rational Evelyn. "Never mind about Germany. Close the door, you're on your own, in your own home, with your husband, your kids. What goes on outside is their business. You have to take care of your inner life. You're nearly forty (I was thirty-four), you're pregnant, face it, I wouldn't give two lirot you'll ever find another man you really care for. Love, it's a seller's market everywhere, you know that."

"All the time, you've been telling me how pretty I am!"

"You are pretty, but you don't know it and you'll never know it. You've got the goods but how can anyone tell? You never put them in the window for display! But that isn't what matters. You're nearly forty, (again!). You've missed most of the boats. Besides, do you know how rare it is? To find love? Most people just settle for shared interests, compatibility. Most women marry only because they don't want to go on living alone. If you've found love, don't just hold on to it, grab it, never let it go! It's like plutonium, there isn't very much around."

It was and it wasn't what I wanted to hear. She hadn't told me anything I didn't know. I suppose all I wanted was a hug, a kiss, a reassurance that she was there for me.

I got that, too. If I needed help, if I needed money... I hugged my perfect Evelyn and told her I would write to her and decided that I would keep regularly in touch.

She was a jewel, and if I preferred zircons to diamonds, it was my bad luck.

Just before I left, she slipped a cheque into my hand.

"What's that for? I don't need money."

"A wedding present, of course."

"But I can't spend lirot over there. What could I do with it?"

She went red. "Get yourself a return ticket." She added hastily, "Just in case."

19. PALESTINE, 1947-8

"The sanatorium to which they sent me was in the hills just outside of Jerusalem, the best climate of all, they said, for curing T.B."
"Was it like the one in Switzerland?"
"It was almost the same. There was the Herr Direktor - we called him 'Herr Professor'. Bed rest. Lying out on balconies. Don't talk. This time, they let me read, though. They had a library of books in Hebrew, Yiddish, English, German, French. I read everything they had in German. So they got me more. I hadn't read a book since I was thirteen. It was a joy."
"What authors?"
"A lot of translations. I read all of Shakespeare. I read Adam's Wealth of Nations. I would have read the telephone book."
"What did you like best?"
"I liked everything. I had a special feeling for Katherine Mansfield. I suppose because she, too, had TB. I found some German writers. Franz Werfel, Hans Fallada and others. Most of them were Jews."
"And you got better?"
"Oh yes, I got better. For some reason, I was less penicillin-resistant. In three months, I was already having dining room privileges. I was negative. I could go for walks."
"What were the other patients like?" I remembered I had asked this question before. So did Rachel.
"Oh they were entirely different. No rich kids, of course, at all. Mostly ex-refugees, like me. From the Camps. We all spoke German, or Yiddish - there were many patients from Poland, and Russia, who spoke mostly Yiddish. There were more older people than in Switzerland. Quite a few had spent the war years in Siberia, escaping from Poland. There was a boy who had lived for four years hidden in a hole under a pigsty; fed by a Polish widow farmer. He was almost blind."
"Didn't you learn any Hebrew?"
"Only a few words. Only the staff spoke Hebrew. I had good intentions, I bought myself a grammar book but it was so dull! I tell you, I wanted to live! I didn't have any self discipline. I wanted it all to happen to me, without my having to do anything at all, and I wanted it right now. Like a child."

"Were you interested in men?"

"I was interested in everything. But I was afraid of men."

"Sex?"

"I never let myself think about sex. It was a forbidden subject. You don't know what TB is like; you're euphoric, always a bit excited. They think it's the slight fever, and the knowing, all the time, you might die soon. So I thought of being a kibbutznik, and, vaguely, there was a husband, and children even, presumably created by immaculate conception. The husband was a sort of younger Dr Bar Zait, a father, a companion, a work-mate, a nurse. I never saw us in bed. I wanted to go to Hanita, the kibbutz the Captain belonged to. It was the only name I knew.

Just like before, the Herr Direktor sent for me. He, too, reminded me of my father. Cultured German accent, very sure of himself. But they weren't at all alike really. Probably every older man reminded me of my father. I still hated him, but I was beginning to be able to miss him."

"You hated him? Why?"

"Because he was a German. He said so. He never wanted to be anything else but one of them."

"'Rachel, (we were all on first name terms) as far as we're concerned, you're cured. You can go!'

"'When?'

"'The sooner, the better. God knows we need the bed. Any relatives or friends?'

"'No. I'd like to go to a kibbutz. Hanita.'

"'I'm sure that can be arranged. But not yet. First a year, maybe only half a year, in Jerusalem. No work for the time being. We have arranged for you to stay with a very nice young couple. Both of them are immigrants from America, you'll like them. Take walks. Get to know the city. Best air in the country, mountain air. Cafés, cinemas, plenty to see for a young girl like you.'

"'Do these people know already? Who fixed up all this?'

"'Why, Youth Aliyah, of course. They'll be in charge of you for a time. I'll give you all the names and addresses. If you need advice, or money, or anything. Someone will be along to see you, regularly. You're only a youngster, you know.'

"It was autumn of 1947. I made a calculation. I was still only seventeen.

"They sent me up to Jerusalem in the Sanatorium van, which doubled (or tripled) as an ambulance, a supply vehicle, transport for the staff and for the patients. It was all they had.

"With me went a young fellow from Youth Aliyah, a Department of the Jewish Agency which dealt with the immigration of orphans. It had no lack of clients. He carried his papers in an old army satchel and looked like a farm boy.

"He carried my suitcase too, which contained very little - a nightgown, toothbrush, a skirt, blouse and sweaters, sanitary pads and so on, all courtesy of WIZO, the Women's Zionist Organisation. None of the clothes were new. Before we set off, he handed me money. 'We're opening a bank account in your name. They'll send you the papers. We'll deposit a cheque every month. We can actually do this only till you're eighteen, then you don't belong to us any more. You belong to another Department of the Jewish Agency. But we'll try to keep you on our own books till you're settled, or God help us all! The bureaucracy, it drives you nuts!'

"'Your board and lodging are paid for. But there are clothes, fares, all the rest. You're not supposed to work, I don't know about going to Hebrew classes and suchlike; we do provide them. Ask the doctor.'

"I didn't. That could come later. 'Suchlike' was probably Youth Movement activities. I felt too old for these. I wanted to be on my own.

"It turned out that only one of the 'nice young couple' was from America. Sara was a fifth generation Jerusalemite, and proud of it, came from a well-based family and had been sent to study at Columbia University in New York. Her husband, Dan, was a true New Yorker. He had been brought up in a religious home, studied in a Yeshiva. As a result, he spoke Hebrew fluently, but with an atrocious accent. Meeting the secular Sara had knocked all religious belief out of his system, leaving only the love of Zion.

"Marrying Sara and going to live with her in Jerusalem was his unquestioned fate. He became a passionate atheist, ate ham and other forbidden delights and was mourned by his parents as if he were dead.

"They lived in a two room apartment in the old district of Yemin Moshe. Later, when I asked them why they had taken me in, they looked at me in amazement. It was self-evident. 'Because we have two rooms, of course!' Space, like everything else, was fully employed.

"My first meeting with Sara was brief. As I arrived, she was leaving.

"'Omigod,' she said, 'I have to go, I simply have to go.' I understood this, it was obvious, although she spoke in English, which was the language she and Dan spoke when they were on their own.

"She then explained, in Hebrew, to my escort, who explained it to me, that she would be back in a few hours, there was a spare key for me on the dining-room table, plenty of food, the bed was made up, feel free. She didn't know when Dan would get in and goodbye for now. As she left, she added, addressing me directly, 'Welcome!' which, in literal translation from the Hebrew, comes out in the beautiful phrase, 'Blessed be she who comes.'

"I registered only two things about Sara. She was gorgeous and she was heavily pregnant; I reckoned about seven months.

"Dan came in about an hour later. To my relief, he spoke fluent Yiddish, which was near enough German for me to understand. He was unshaven and dirty, and looked as if he had slept outdoors.

"This, I soon found out, was typical of how they lived. Each came and went; they were seldom at home, not even at night, and even less often, together. Yet that they were deeply in love, there was no doubt. They spoke to, looked at, only each other, across a roomful of guests.

"I never found out what Dan's job was. They saw a lot of people. They always invited me in, but only afterwards, after a lot of talk.

"Sara did come back, a few hours later. I stared at her in unbelieving shock. She was no longer pregnant. How had she lost the child? She understood immediately, laughed, and lifted up her skirt. There was a huge pocket sewn into it, inside, on the front. 'I was carrying hand grenades,' she explained. Many women did it. The British were less inclined to search pregnant women than others.

"The Jews were building up stocks of whatever arms they could get, for the big confrontation, when the British went. It was only a question of time.

"They were buried in secret hideouts, usually dug-outs, called slicks, which were sometimes found by the British, who considered it a serious crime and punished it accordingly.

"The Jews weren't in any situation to be choosy about weapons. They accepted anything. Once Sara smuggled two small exquisite duelling pistols. They were genuine antiques. She didn't have to tell me to keep my mouth shut. I was one of them. I hardly ever saw Sara, or Dan, but they were close, like family.

"Because I was so much alone, I went out a great deal. Sun, I had been told, was good for me, but not too much of it, so I chose shady streets. I sat for long hours in cafés, nursing a cup of herbal tea, watching the people go by. They were endlessly fascinating.

"There wasn't a type or a part of the world that wasn't represented. They spoke in a hundred foreign tongues. Only the young people spoke Hebrew.

"I fell in love with Jerusalem, of course. Who doesn't? I loved to wander in the Old City. At that time, Jews and Arabs, on the individual level, were friendly, there were even intimate friendships.

"The vendors greeted me. 'Oh what a lovely young girl! For you, I give it,' ('it' could be anything, from fresh-baked pittas to hand-hammered copper pots) 'for nothing. Only one pound.'

"One day, only a couple of weeks after I arrived in Jerusalem, I was standing looking up at the Western Wall, when a young man came out of a house nearby. He stared at me, then came up and invited me at first in Hebrew, but then by hand signals, to have a cup of coffee with him.

"He was handsome, charming and polite. He placed a hand under my elbow, only indicating, hardly touching; with delicate reverence, he led me away, unresisting. I was lonely. Why ever not? He talked all the time. I didn't understand a word of it. When he realised I didn't understand Hebrew, he switched to mime. He was a natural. He pointed to a woman passing by, a fat woman, imitating her walk. A curve of the hand outlined her body. 'Woman,' he said, 'fat.' He had switched to Arabic. He was an Arab.

"We went to a café in the new city, because in the old one, men drank only with men. Arab women stayed at home most of the time, going out only to shop for food. Even their dresses were bought for them by their men.

"We stopped at a café I had come to know. Most of the patrons were elderly German Jews, people who no longer worked, widowers, mostly, who came to play chess. It was brown and dark and orderly, and had straight-backed uncomfortable chairs. There were a few women too, mostly alone, with shopping baskets, dog-tired, a short rest before going back to the housework and the kids, and probably a part-time job on the side. It was a hard-working country.

"My friend pointed to himself. 'Sami,' he said, and pointed to me. 'Rachel.'

"We then shook hands.

"He got out a pencil and paper, and gave them to me. 'Table,' he said, in Arabic, and made me write the word down, in transliteration, of course. 'Chair'. 'Waiter'. 'Coffee'. 'Tea'. 'Handbag'. 'Book'. 'Newspaper'. 'Shopping cart'. In the end, I had ten words of Arabic. He made me understand I was to learn them that night. He would meet me tomorrow, indicating his watch, at the same time and place. He bought me a notebook and a pen.

"We took to meeting every day. Each time, he taught me more words. Then phrases, and sentences. I enjoyed learning. I enjoyed his interest in me. It was so caring, so respectful and so intense. He was reliable. He always came. He was my only friend: Sara and Dan were sister and brother, but they were seldom there.

"After a few weeks, we could almost converse. Even at that level, it was never boring. He pointed out everything, he mimicked wonderfully; he persisted till I understood.

"In less than three months, I was chatting freely. My notebook was full. I found out that he was a small time import-export man, dealing mainly in cosmetics, non-prescription medicines like aspirins and antacids, and diarrhoea cures for which there was a big demand. He didn't seem to have regular working hours. He spent more and more time with me. We were sometimes whole days together. I took him to meet Sara and Dan and they seemed to get on rather well.

"Then he asked me to marry him. It was totally unexpected. I said, "No." He was my dear, dear friend.

"He had never even kissed me.

"He took my hand, and stroked it gently. I realised I wasn't going to get out of it easily. I tried to explain to him. I had told him about the tuberculosis. My health was now much better. My monthly check-ups were all negative.

"I told him I was going to live on a kibbutz. I told him how important this was to me, how much, in my inmost being, I wanted to live my own, my Jewish life. He listened politely. He understood nothing. It did not make him deviate an inch.

"Time was on his side.

"The British announced that they were giving up the Mandate. They were going to pull out. The Mandate was being handed back to the U.N. The Jews announced that after the pull-out they would proclaim a Jewish State. The surrounding Arab nations prepared to attack.

"In Czechoslovakia a couple of obsolete planes were taken apart and put into bigger planes, to be flown out and reassembled. This was the Jewish air force. It was pitiful.

"Sara and Dan disappeared almost entirely; I was alone most of the time in the flat. It turned out Dan was a Palmach colonel. Sara was caught smuggling hand grenades, spent a few days in prison, then was released. Small fry.

"I decided to go to Hanita, finally; but it was already too late. There was violence. There were ambushes. The road wasn't safe. I was advised to stay where I was. The British were handing over arms to the local Arabs - they expected to be back. A little gratitude would be in order.

"Sami kept at me, he never let it go. 'Rachel, it's hopeless. As soon as the British pull out, the Arab countries will attack. The Syrians will strike from the North. A proper army, with big guns and tanks. Egypt will come up from the South, they have planes, Jordan from the East. There will be none of you left alive. They will drive all the Jews into the sea.'

"'But why?'

"'Because of the Moslem belief - what has been Islam must be forever Islam.' Sami was a Christian, himself. I believed him. Most of the Jews believed this too. They were going to fight to the death, it was their last stand. They had no hope of winning, the odds against were so great. He pointed out to me people in the street.

"'Look at him, he's just off the boat. Look at his boots.' He was a thin kid wearing old Russian army boots. 'He'll be dead in a month. That woman - she's pregnant. She'll never see her kid.'

"'You'll be slaughtered, like rats.'

"I began to dream of Mauthausen and the walking dead. I wanted so much to live. I wanted to be with the Jews, but I didn't want to go down with the Jews. 'Sara and Dan too,' he said, 'Everyone!'

"He made me promises. We would live in Jerusalem. I could have Jewish children, live with them a Jewish life, he didn't care, whatever I wanted, I could have.

"So I married him.

"When the State was proclaimed, that day in May 1948, they sang and danced in the streets all night. There was such joy! The guns would start tomorrow, but that night was theirs.

"It wasn't my joy. I didn't hear the singing and the dancing; I heard the guns.

"Three months later, it was all over; there was a Jewish State, Israel; but I was an Arab wife, locked in an Arab land. The walls were up, the gates were closed, there was no way back.

20. ISRAEL, 1979

Professor Strumpfeld died.
He was bedridden, not in pain, but full of an immense weariness. He just ticked over. Sometimes Rachel read to him, until a thin skeletal hand on her arm indicated he had had enough.

She almost never left him. She had put up a folding bed for herself next to his. She went out only to buy food. And to visit her grandson, once a week.

Once, he roused.
"Rachel," he said, "I want to marry you."
"Don't be a fool."
"Because of the pension. I can't leave you anything else, my ex-wife already got the money, my son gets the house."
"No."
"Why not? It deprives nobody."
"I don't deserve it." She was adamant.

At last a night came, when he said, "You remember your promise? Now."
"How do you want them? In milk, with honey?"
"Any way you like."
"Are you sure?"
"I'm sure."
"It's for you, not for me? I can go on."
"It's for me."

So she crushed twenty sleeping tablets in hot milk and honey and he drank it, holding her hand.
"Stay with me."

She sat there, through the night. His breathing became stertorous, and then stopped. When she was quite sure, she phoned his doctor.

She told me what had happened, in her usual terse way.
I thought about it, then I said, "Don't tell Dr Lustig."
"Why not?"
I didn't explain. I said savagely, "Just don't."

Dr Lustig asked her to stay on until after the mourning period and then till the son took over the house. She agreed. There wasn't much to do and she was restless.

The will had been read. He had left her something after all - his handwritten manuscripts. Famous as he was, perhaps not now, but later, they would be worth something. "A sensitive gesture," said Dr Lustig.

It wasn't just a gesture. There were two unpublished, full length texts in his desk drawer. They would bring in quite a sum. She offered them to the son but he wouldn't look at them. They were the Devil's work he said, he would have nothing to do with them. The son took over the house, and Rachel moved out. Her flat was furnished sparsely. She spent most of her time in libraries, or learning Hebrew. She now spoke fluently enough, but she read only slowly and her spelling was poor. Her pronunciation wasn't good either, because she had few opportunities to speak.

Since she had more time, and since I would be leaving soon, we met more often. Mainly at Hamozeg. We were regulars and had our own table; Avi mostly working late, would grab a sandwich. He didn't mind.

"Any job offers?"
"Yes."
"What?"
"Dr Lustig asked me to be his housekeeper."
"Did you accept?"
"No."
"Why not?"
"Many reasons."

I wasn't going to get anything more.

"Anything else?"
"Yes." She mentioned a famous name. She was a poet and song writer.
"What's the problem?"
"Alzheimer's Disease."
"You didn't want to?"
"No."
"Why not?"
"I don't know if I can. Disease of old age. I never knew old people. It doesn't seem natural to me for people to die of old age."
"So what will you do?"
"Read, study."
"How long can you do that?"
"I saved almost all my salary. At least a year."
"What did you do with the Professor's manuscripts?"
"I gave them to Dr Lustig. He'll get them published."

I breathed a sigh of relief. He would have the sense to invest the money in her name.
"What will you do when your money runs out?"
"There'll be a job. I could go to Hanita."
"You'll apply to be a member?"
"At my age? They wouldn't have me! As a volunteer."

21. JORDAN, 1947-58

When Rachel had told me about her journey to Palestine, about the time she had lived in Palestine, Dr Bar Zait, the sanatorium, Sara and Dan, even Sami's courtship, the narrative had flowed easily; she was a young eager girl again. I hardly had to prompt her at all. Now, when she told me about her life in Jordan, as during her revelations of the Camps, of Dr Brock's death, she clammed up. Then, and now, again, it was the older Rachel speaking. She replied to my questions briefly. She volunteered little. The young girl, wounded, but still open, wanting so much to live, had metamorphosed again into this ageless woman; taciturn, closed. She still wanted to live, alright, but in a different way. Not for pleasure, perhaps not for fulfilment, even; just a job that had to be done.

"Were you happy with Sami?"
"No. I realised immediately it was a mistake."
"What did you do?"
"I asked him to let me go back."
"Back?"
"For a couple of months there was fighting, but Jews were still living in the Old City. The gates were open. They were holding them in the South, pushing them back in the North. They had a chance."
"How did you know?"
"Sara came to visit me. Often. She knew."
"Why didn't you just leave?"
"He kept me locked in the house. He said it was for my safety. Perhaps it was."
"How did he treat you?"
"He was kind. But he was the husband. An Arab husband. His word was law."
"Couldn't Sara help you?"
"How? Besides, he was right. She was killed."
"And Dan?"
"Dan, too. At Latrun."
There were heavy losses at Latrun.
"What did you do all day?"
"At first, he was there a lot. He went on teaching me Arabic. He taught me to be an Arab wife."

"Which was?"

"We lived with his sister. Cleaning, preparing their kind of food. She did the shopping. He wouldn't let me out, even into the street. He was afraid for me. He was afraid, too, that I would go back."

"Did you get on with her?"

"No."

"He began to be away at times?"

"More and more. Sometimes days at a time."

"What was he doing?"

"Who knows? Maybe working. Maybe helping to fight the Jews."

"He wasn't a soldier?"

"No, but he had a lot of information. Maybe he just gave the authorities information. He had to. It would be expected of him."

"How long did this go on?"

"It seemed a long time. Until after the battle for the Old City. I saw it all. From the roof. There was a flat roof. I used it a lot. I saw the fighting. I saw the Jews leave. I lost my head. I screamed 'Take me with you!' His sister told him I wasn't behaving properly."

"What did he do?"

"He forbade me to go on the roof. He told me I was an Arab wife and that he was ashamed of me. I had to think only of him."

"And then?"

"The Jews were driven out. The Jordanian army was there. They built a wall between the old and new cities. There was no way back."

"Were you resigned?"

"Not then. I fought him."

"How did he react?"

"He laughed. He said I needed a child. I told him, 'Never!'"

"But you did have a child?"

"I hadn't a chance. He got me pregnant immediately."

"How was sex?"

"Painful. I was always dry."

"Didn't he notice?"

"It seemed to him natural. Arab women weren't supposed to enjoy sex. It was like older times."

"Did he mind that you weren't a virgin?"

"We never spoke of it."

"Were you glad to have the child?"

"I tried to lose it. I threw myself down the stairs. It didn't work. All I did was break my wrist."

"Was there any change, after the war was over?"

"Not much. There was the wall. The police were very suspicious. They thought I might be a spy. They came often, but they were fairly polite. His sister disliked me more than ever. She said the marriage was shameful."

"Was it better after you had the child?"

"It was better. Even though it was a girl, he was so pleased. The baby enchanted him. He was pleased with me. He let me call her Sara. He kept his word, it was a Jewish name."

"So Sara was your first child? How long did all this go on?"

"For a time. He let me go out. It was safe. I couldn't get away. I had no papers, no passport, the borders were closed to me. I was a wife: I couldn't go anywhere without his permission."

"Were you unhappy?"

"I was frantic."

"Next? What happened next?"

"He got me pregnant again."

"You didn't want that?"

"No. I still hoped I'd get away. I thought that with one child it wouldn't be impossible. With two, I'd never make it. It was a dream. There wasn't any way out, even without any children at all."

"Didn't you have any rights?"

"Women didn't have rights in their society."

"Why did you have a second child?"

"It happened."

"Did you still love him?"

"I never loved him."

"Did you still like him, then?"

"Sometimes. He apologised. He was like a grown-up child."

"You had another girl?"

"He wasn't pleased. Still, he loved the children. He played with them."

"Did you love them?"

A long pause.

"I felt responsible for them. I took great care of them, I thought of them all the time. Is that love?"

I couldn't answer her. "After that, he left? Did you see it coming?"

"No. He went out to work most days. I hardly noticed when he was there. Then one day he told me:
"'I'm going to Kuwait. I have an offer of a good job.'
"'When?'
"'Tomorrow.'
"'Am I going with you?'
"'Not at present. You'll stay here. I'll send you money.' The next day, he was gone, early, I was still asleep. It had never occurred to me he would take the girls."
"What did you do?"
"I went to the authorities. I wanted my children. I asked them for a permit to go to Kuwait. They asked me if I had my husband's permission. I told them about the girls. They were just babies. Sara was three, Dana was only two. They explained to me that I had no rights, didn't I know that? Then someone came in and recognised me. 'It's the Jewish woman.' They sent me back. They told his sister, Yasmin, she'd have to look after me better. Yasmin's husband was now my guardian, till Sami came back, they said."
"Yasmin had a husband?"
"Oh yes. She was twenty-four, she had six kids."
"Did your husband write to you?"
"As if nothing had happened. He was fine, the children were fine. He sent money."
"Did you answer him?"
"I pleaded for the girls. I gave the letters to Yasmin. I didn't even have his address. I don't know whether she sent them on or not."
"And this went on?"
"For years. Then the money stopped. I didn't hear from him at all. Yasmin said I would have to go."
"'Where?' I asked. 'Where could I go?'
"'What do I care?'
"I went to his parents' home, in Hebron. I thought they might get him to send for me; to give me news of the girls. I didn't want him, but I wanted the girls.
"His mother was quite kind. They lived in a very big, fancy house, with two other of his brothers' families. She said he had probably divorced me. After all, it was eight years... She told me to forget about him and the children. She couldn't take me in, I didn't

belong to the family any more, but she felt some obligation. She would help me find a job. What could I do?

"'Do you type?'

"'No.'

"'Well then, we'll have to find you a cleaning job. You look very strong.'

"I was. The years of inactivity had done wonders. I didn't have TB any more."

"Where did she send you?"

"She took me to the town hospital. She talked to the Staff Manager. I got the job. Very small salary, but a room."

"Was that unusual?"

"Yes. She didn't want me on her hands. He did her a favour."

"You took it?"

"What else could I do?"

"When was this?"

"I guess it was about 1958. I stayed there for twenty years."

"Why didn't you come here earlier? Why did you wait so long? Why not in 1967, when Hebron was already Israeli-occupied territory?"

"It's a long story."

"Tell me."

But at this point, she stopped. We would not see each other for a week; Rachel was going to Hanita, to pick apples. They had advertised for volunteers.

"Why only a week?"

"Because of the boy."

She came back, very tanned. We went for a walk together, along the Tel Aviv promenade. Big American-style ice cream parlours. Town life.

"How was it?"

"Good."

"As you imagined?"

"No. I still thought of it as it would have been in 1948. Not much food... Hard, back-breaking work. Living in tents. Fetching water in buckets from a well. Work by day, guard by night. Of course it isn't at all like that."

It hadn't been like that even in 1948.

Now, well fed people lived in well-built flats. A modest measure of prosperity. Television sets in every home. A theatre, a swimming pool. The comrades worked in a factory, or pressed buttons to irrigate and fertilise the mechanised fields. Tractors, not the hands of people, dug up stones. Harvesters. Even the cows were computerised. Water came out of taps and flowed to the fields under automatic control through irrigation drips. There were still the kibbutz values, but it was no longer a joyous, hard pioneering life, stirring, because it was so hard. From Hanita, at least, that had gone forever, she would never get it back.

"So you worked in the Hebron Hospital. Just cleaning?"

"Mostly. Sweeping, dusting, washing floors. When they were busy, which was nearly always, I took the patients their food trays, and emptied bed pans."

"Was it a good hospital?"

"I had no standards of comparison. Middling, I guess. It was a small town."

"Were you," I hesitated over the word 'happy' - "content?"

"I was never content. I wanted the girls. I wanted my life, my Jewish life. I wanted to go back. I always wanted that."

"But, at the hospital?"

"I didn't mind the work. His mother gave me some money before she left. I bought myself a radio. And somehow she got the police off my back. Nobody knew I was Jewish. No-one bothered me at all any more. My wages were a pittance. Everything went on food."

"Didn't they feed you?"

"Hospital patients' food. It's all the same, farina, semolina, couscous, pudding. Mushes, whatever you call it. When they knew me better, they gave me the run of the ward kitchen. Olives, dates, yoghurt, what the nurses ate. Pork chops, too." She smiled.

"Didn't you mind, always being with sick people, with the dying?"

"It seemed natural to me."

"What did you do after your work was finished?"

"I started at five, had breakfast, worked until two. After lunch I was usually tired, I slept. In the evening, I worked again, cleaning up after the visiting hours. Then I was really tired. I listened to the radio and went to bed."

"That was it?"

"That's all there was. But I lived a Jewish life."

"How?"

"I observed the festivals. I didn't eat bread during the nine days of Passover. I fasted on Yom Kippur. Later, I planted a tree on Tu B'Shvat."

"Where?"

"In Israel. In the north."

"How did you know the dates of the festivals? How could you plant a tree?"

"I guessed the dates. I made rough calculations. Sometimes, I heard about them on the radio. The Jordanians were very interested in Jewish affairs - Israeli ones, rather. They distinguished between Israelis and Jews."

"So apart from missing the girls, you were content?"

"I wasn't unhappy. I missed books. There was nothing to be found in German, even if I had had the money to buy books. Only Arabic and English."

"Was your room pleasant?"

"It was more like a large cupboard. It had been a store room. Just enough room for a bed, a table and a chair. It had a window though."

"How did you plant the tree?"

"A few years after I had started working, they brought in a woman, a foreigner. She had been on a trip to Abraham's tomb and had fallen and broken her leg."

"You got to know her?"

I was jealous of everyone she knew.

"She said to me one morning, I was sweeping under her bed, 'Hey, you. Speak English, French?'

"'No.'

"'German?'

Reluctantly, 'Yes.'

"'Gott sei Dank.'

"She released a flood of German. I was sorry for her. She was a Swiss schoolteacher, an elderly woman, near sixty, I would think."

"Married?"

"A widow. Husband had died recently. Heart attack. The trip was to help her get over it. Even without the accident, it didn't. She talked about him all the time."

"So you talked to her a lot?"

"When I brought her supper tray. Sometimes I sat with her at night."

"You told her you were Jewish?"

"It was obvious my native tongue was German. It wasn't hard to guess."

"You told her about your marriage?"

"Yes."

"About Mauthausen? About Dr Brock?"

"No, not that. I never spoke to her about Germany."

"How long was she at the hospital?"

"A long time. They had to break her leg and set it again. Then an infection set in. It was only a small hospital. They weren't great experts."

"Didn't you advise her to go somewhere else?"

"It wasn't possible. For a long time she couldn't be moved. In the end, the Swiss Ambassador's wife came up from Amman. She had her flown out."

"So you only knew her a few months?"

"It was enough."

"Did you keep in touch?"

"For years. She sent me books. There was a parcel every two or three weeks. She consulted with the Head of the Jewish Community in Zurich. She went there especially, she lived in a small town. They drew up a list. She gave him the money, he bought them and sent them out. Occasionally, she sent me books directly. Novels. She sent money every year to the Jewish National Fund to plant two trees on Tu B'Shvat; one for her and one for me."

"What was her name?"

"Sophie?"

"She wasn't Jewish?"

"No. Her family was French. She had been brought up in the German speaking canton, though, it was her first language."

"Couldn't she have got you out? To Switzerland?"

"She tried. The Embassy told her to leave it alone. I was an Arab wife. They couldn't rock the boat."

"Weren't you divorced, by then?"

"If so, I didn't know it."

"Did she help you find the girls?"

"That was too dangerous. For them. Also for me."

"Are you still in touch with her?"

"She died. But the Zurich people went on sending me books. There was TV now, too. Someone gave one of the wards a set as a gift. I saw a lot of Israel. Only the bad news, of course, it was slanted. But I made allowances for that."

"Did time pass slowly?"

"I hardly knew how it went. I had work, I had books."

"Did you have friends?"

"You always ask the same foolish questions. I never had friends!"

"Wasn't Sophie a friend?"

"I hardly knew her. She didn't know me. She was sorry for me."

22. ISRAEL, 1979

Rachel was offered another job. A young kid, a boy of fourteen, with cystic fibrosis. Name of Udi. The parents were separated, the father abroad on a very special mission. His wife hadn't told him about the family genes.

The mother needed hospitalisation, she had paranoid episodes. Not a Holocaust victim, just an unstable woman from Iraq. The father was from South America, spoke Spanish. Big arms deals.

Nobody knew what to do with the boy. There were plenty of Iraqi relatives. He would have none of it. Said give him a housekeeper and he'd manage on his own till one or another of the parents came back.

Rachel's Hebrew was good enough now. She met the boy, Dr Lustig brought them together. He was intelligent, charming and very ill. They liked each other at first sight.

"What do you think of her?"
"She doesn't fuss."
"Do you like the boy?"
"Yes. Would he be willing to meet my grandson? Talk to him a bit?"
"Ask him."
He would.

The kid's home was in Jerusalem, which was, of course, handy for Rachel. Everything was breaking up. I, too, was going away. Further, much further. There would be only Dr Lustig left in Tel Aviv, minding the office.

I asked Dr Lustig, "What are the kid's chances?"
"Practically nil, short of some new treatment. Or a miracle."
"Why do you always give her the hard ones?"
"That's all we have."
"How long?"
"Nobody knows."

Rachel settled in. They had a huge flat in Jerusalem, the first floor of an old Arab home, with a courtyard, and a well.

I called her.
"You know I'm leaving next week. Sunday."
"So soon?"

"I'd like to invite you to a farewell dinner, very splashy. King David Hotel, perhaps. Would you come? Tomorrow?"

"I can't leave the boy."

"So make it lunch, then, and bring Udi along. Bring your grandson too, if you like." I thought the boys could entertain each other and leave Rachel for me.

"I don't think he could go out. He's coughing a lot."

"I want to see you."

Laughing. "You mean you want your pound of flesh. He likes Chinese food. There's a take-away nearby, we could eat here. Would that do?"

"I'll pick the food up on my way. Your grandson too?"

"I'll try."

She told me where the take-away was and we agreed I'd drive up the following day.

Udi was an appealing person. He wasn't exactly a child: the eyes that looked out of that thin brown face knew suffering and approaching death, were wise with hospital stays and consultations, treatments and talk and the cessation of talk. There was a wheelchair, but he wasn't in it.

You were immediately aware of the harmony between Udi and Rachel. Comradeship. The grandson was there too, Mahmoud. I asked him his age. He said, "Thirteen," and looked at Rachel. That meant he was past Bar Mitzvah age. She had told him, he knew he was a Jew, according to Jewish religious law. He wasn't comfortable; he couldn't deal with Udi and the cystic fibrosis and the strange house and me.

He probably couldn't deal with the new knowledge that he was technically not Arab, and it wasn't apparent whether he could deal with Rachel. He had presumably his father's brown eyes, but otherwise the resemblance to Rachel was striking. He must have noticed it. He wasn't a very mature thirteen. He looked scared. But then he had good reason to be, caught between a Jewish grandmother and parents who were PLO.

When Rachel spoke to him, he listened attentively. An obedient child. Polite. Maybe more than that; the frightened glances were also full of respect. She had given him a formidable heritage. He took her very seriously indeed.

I had brought a lot of food. Boyish appetites.

Udi, the Chinese food lover, only picked at his. He was coughing a great deal. Mahmoud ate politely, also without much appetite. He was caught up in his huge divergent realities.

Rachel and I did our best to cope with the rest.

After the meal, I cleared up the plates and cartons. Rachel said to Udi: "Exercises."

"I don't feel up to it."

"You won't have to do anything. I'll do it all. You just have to breathe."

"I'm not sure that I want to," quietly.

"I want you to."

Their looks met. "All right," he said and they went off.

As I cleaned up, I talked to Mahmoud, the usual conversation between an adult stranger and a child - where he went to school and what subjects he liked.

But he had questions of his own.

"How long have you known her?"

"Who?"

"Rachel." Then, with difficulty, "my grandmother."

"Not long. Not much more than a year." He made it seem like forever.

"She's pretty formidable, isn't she?" He spoke Hebrew, of course. But it was his second language. Sometimes he had difficulty finding a word.

"What do you mean?"

"Well, she knows so much. Whatever you ask her, she knows the answer." This was not the terse, monosyllabic Rachel I knew.

"For example?"

"About history. Ancient history of all peoples. Of course, especially of the Jews."

"That interests you?"

"She makes it interesting. And then I'm Jewish, you know."

"Are you sure? How do you feel about it?"

"Confused. And then I have to keep it secret from my father. That bothers me."

"Does it bother you that you are a Jew?"

"I don't think so. It's something to be proud of, isn't it?"

"Does your father hate the Jews?"

"He admires them. He says we're cousins, it's strictly a land dispute. We have them all the time. But he wants them out of

Palestine." I hoped he would always see it in that simplistic way. Rachel had put a big burden on these thin shoulders.

"Do you think it was right of Rachel to tell you that you were a Jew?"

He looked at me in astonishment. "But of course she was right. I'm entitled."

It was in a way a very big, a very adult statement. I looked at him with respect.

Rachel came back.

"Udi's sorting his stamp collection upstairs. Do you want to help him?" Mahmoud nodded, and went.

Rachel made coffee, strong, thick, black, sweet, the way I hated. She was a little distant. Her eyes saw through walls; her two boys, getting to know each other.

I took my coffee and poured it into a larger cup, added hot water and milk and sat down firmly.

"Rachel?"

"Your pound of flesh?"

"Rachel," I said, "Part of my life has always been missing, the one part that would make sense of all the rest."

"I know."

But it was still like pulling teeth, like being straight man to the comic, except that it wasn't funny; it was tragic and bitter, all her lost years.

23. JORDAN, 1963-78, ISRAEL, 1979

"When did Sophie die?"
"It must have been about 1963."
"And immediately after that you met your second husband?"
"Not immediately. I don't remember exactly when. He was in and out of hospital so often."
"What brought you together?"
"He was mostly in for tests, at first. He was ambulatory. He was bored. He liked to talk. I was always around."
"Did you like him?"
"Well enough. Not especially, He was dignified. He was old."
"How old?"
"When he first started coming in - about fifty, I suppose."
"What did you talk about?"
"Nothing much. At first."
"When did it change?"
"The police started coming again. It was awkward, they could come at any hour. He asked me what was wrong."
"So you told him?"
"A bit, yes."
"What did he say?"
"That he would try to help me."
"And did he?"
"Yes. Again, they stopped coming. They left me alone."
"Were you relieved?"
"The interrogations were not pleasant. They were convinced I was a spy."
"So you continued to see him?"
"At the hospital. He was in every few months. He had vomiting, and pain. They thought it was his gall bladder. Twice they decided to operate, but each time, he improved."
"And then?"
"The Staff Director sent for me. He said I would have to go. I asked why. 'Because I was Jewish.'
"'But you've known I was Jewish all the time.'
"'Times are now difficult. I am personally sorry, you are a good worker. I sincerely hope you find another job. I can give you two weeks.'

"Saoud was hospitalised at the time.
"'What's the matter?'
"I wasn't crying, but I was near to it. I had become soft and forgotten suffering. It was so unfair."
"You told him?"
"Yes."
"What did he say?"
"He thought for a moment or two. 'I'll marry you.'
"'You're married already.'
"'I am a Moslem. We are allowed four wives.'
"'How would it help?'
"'I come from a very influential family. We are related to the King. I am not rich, but I am a member of the Royal family. No-one would meddle with my wife. And I could try to help you find your girls.'
"What did you answer?"
"I couldn't. I didn't want to marry again. One mistake was enough. He said: 'I am not a well man. I am not proposing a sexual union. I will simply give you my protection. You may continue to work and live here if you wish. I will help you in any way I can. The marriage will mean nothing. But without it I doubt if you can avoid imprisonment.'
"So what did you do?"
"I married him. What choice did I have?"
"Did it work out well?"
"It wasn't a marriage at all. On the wedding night, he asked me to stay with him so as not to put him to shame. He never touched me. The next day, I went back to the hospital."
"And life went on, as before?"
"It was better. The Staff Manager apologised. He raised my wages. I never saw the police."
"And your husband?"
"Saoud? He was a man of his word. He found my daughters for me. Both were married. Dana was still in Kuwait, but Sara was in East Jerusalem."
"Did you go to see Sara?"
"Saoud told me not to. She was married to a very important man. A Palestinian. It could be very dangerous for her."
"And after that?"

"At the end of 1966, they sent him to the Amman hospital for further tests. They found out at last what was wrong with him. He had cancer of the liver, an atypical one, very rare. They couldn't operate."

"He knew?"

"He knew. They told him he had only a year to live, maybe two."

"And you? In 1967, after the Six Days' War, when Hebron was Israeli-occupied, why didn't you cross over then?"

"I didn't want to leave him. He had done a lot for me. It was a debt."

"Didn't he have family?"

"He had a wife and grown up children."

"Tthey didn't visit him at the hospital?"

"They visited him all the time. But he also needed me."

"When did he die?"

"He hung on for years. He was in and out of hospital. Surgery. Radiation therapy. It ruined him. Periodically, he had to send the family to his brother in Amman. He had hardly any money left."

"So he relied on you?"

"He told me a thousand times: 'Go over to your own people. Don't stay for me.' He never thought of himself."

"And you never saw your daughter?"

"Oh yes, I did. I had her name, so I got her address out of the telephone book."

"Did you call on her? How did she greet you?"

"I went to the house. It was very large, imposing, very well kept up. She answered the door. 'What can I do for you?'

"I am your mother."

"'What! You're insane. My mother died a few years after I was born.'

"'Look at me.'

"If it wasn't for her eyes, Sami's eyes, for the age difference, she could have been my twin."

"She said, 'Come in.'

"It was a very floridly furnished house. Big furniture. Big floral prints. A lot of ornaments. Everything looked rich and new.

"I said: 'You're my daughter, Sara.'

"'That isn't my name.'

"'It was. What is it now?

"'Yasmin. After an aunt of mine who died. Who are you?'
"I told her a bit. Where I came from. About the time in Jerusalem with Sami, when she was born."
"'Where do you live?'
"I told her.
"I asked her: 'Is your father alive?'
"'Yes. He's in Kuwait. He's a building contractor. He brings in workers from Korea and Portugal. He's doing very well.'
"'And your sister?'
"'Nuria? She's a social worker in Kuwait.'
"'Her name was Dana. Is she married?'
"'Yes. To another social worker. They have two kids. Sara's a Jewish name. Am I Jewish?'
"'You have a Jewish mother. So according to Jewish Law, yes.'
"'Oh my God! O Jesus save me, he'll divorce me. He'll send me away.'
"Your husband? Doesn't he love you? Why does it matter so much?"
"'He's Arafat's right-hand man! They'd never trust him. It would be the end for him. He'd never forgive me. He'd get rid of me.' She was hysterical.
"I said: 'Sara, I'll never tell. I would never spoil your life. If you're happy, just go on. Do you have children?'
"'One boy. He's four.'
"'All I want of you is, let me see the boy. On my day off. Let me take him out.'
"'Why?'
"'He's my grandson. Just this one child. You'll have others.'
"'I'll never have another. He's the first and last.'
"'Why?'
"'I had a hysterectomy. My husband doesn't know. He'd send me away for that, too.'
"'How could you hide it?'
"'He's never here. He's in Tunis, Lebanon, Europe, you name it. He's a liaison man. He's almost never at home.'
"'Isn't he interested in his son?'
"'He brings him presents.'
"I looked around. There was a huge rocking-horse. It was suitable for a boy of ten!
"'Like that?'

"She flushed.
"'He's a political. He's not a family man.'
"'It doesn't sound like much of a life for you.'
"'It's not bad. There's money. Everyone looks up to me. It's the best I can do.'
"'Is it what you wanted?'
"'No. I wanted to be educated. My father wouldn't let me. School wasn't compulsory for girls. I never learned to read or write. I wanted to be independent. I wanted a job.'
"'What did you want to be?'
"'A short-hand typist.'
"I put my arms round her. She pulled away. She was hostile, still very suspicious.
"'All you want is to see the boy?' She thought it was blackmail.
"'Only once a week. I'll take him out. Your husband won't know.'
"'What do you want him for? You want him to become a Jew, don't you? You want to take him away.'
"'No! But he has to have a choice. When he is older.'
"What could she do? She wasn't interested in me. She was deathly afraid of me. She thought it was the price for not giving her away.
"She said, 'Why was I called Sara?'
"'After a girl I knew that died.'
"'And Dana?'
"'After her husband. He was also killed. At Latrun.'
"She agreed. Just as long as I kept out of her life. That's how it is. She had no idea you always lose your children, anyway."
"Did Saoud die?"
"He hung on for a long time. Years. It was no life. He had many operations. They kept patching him up."
"And you?"
"I was seeing the boy every week. He was a nice kid. We got on very well. Then Saoud died. And I crossed over to the other side."
"Immediately?"
"After a few years."
It was too fluent. Her hands, too, betrayed her.
I said: "That wasn't all."
Reluctantly; "It was a punishment."

A long pause. It was over. I had never been just a 'listener'. I had lived with Rachel through the years of her life. I waited now for some great revelation. Nothing happened. We sat there together, separate, silent. I had endured all her experiences; but they told me nothing at all.

At this point Mahmoud came into the room. He sat down beside Rachel. He laid his hand on hers. It was a gesture at once commanding and supportive. It was a very Arab gesture. She was his.

"What do you want to do when you're grown up?" I asked him.

"I'm nearly fourteen. I am grown up."

"Well, not legally, you know."

"When I'm sixteen, I'll be legally free to leave home."

"And what will you do?"

"Join a kibbutz."

"And if they accept you? Is there anything special you want to be?"

"I'd want to study, too, medicine perhaps. And of course, I'd be able to bring my grandmother to live in the kibbutz with me."

"Any particular kibbutz?"

He stared at me. "Hanita, of course."

Rachel started.

"No!"

Sulkily: "I thought it would please you!" He was just a little boy.

"It wouldn't please me for you to live my life. You have to live your own. Hanita is *my* life."

"What if I wanted to stay an Arab?"

"Whatever you choose. Whatever you feel is right."

"And you'd still be my grandmother?"

"Why not?"

He looked relieved. I didn't think he wanted to join a kibbutz, or fight in the Army, or be a doctor, even; I didn't think he wanted a Jewish life.

He was like his mother, whose whole life's ambition had been no more than to work in an office; to be a secretary, ordered about by the boss, at everybody's beck and call. He would want things to go on, safely, just as they had always done. He was a fearful child, afraid of his powerful father. Like his mother, he too would want to work in an office, some low management job, little responsibility, a small but respectable degree of independence. His grandmother would be the daring adventure, the big secret, what made him different from the others and justified his choice. She did all the dangerous living for him. He was part of her. She was in his life. He needed no more.

I think Rachel knew this.

I looked at her. Our thoughts were similar.

She shrugged her shoulders. If not in this child...

Mahmoud went home, deflated, but probably much easier in his mind. Rachel went off to take care of Udi. I heard her in the kitchen, the sizzling of milk being poured from a pot, her low voice intermingling with his, the footsteps upstairs, the coughing - still audible - becoming less frequent; then silence.

Presumably he had fallen asleep. Did he wake during the night, did she get up to go and sit with him, talk to him or just lay a hand on his, till he fell asleep again? Probably. She would do everything that needed to be done. Would he become the child she truly loved, her Jewish child, this dark intelligent boy who would certainly be dead before he reached his twenties, who probably had only a couple of years to live?

She came back to the table and sat down beside me.

I went back to what had been bothering me.

"Why was it a punishment? What were you being punished for? Who was punishing you?"

She looked at me in amazement.

"I was punishing myself, of course."

"But why?"

"I wasn't fit to live."

"Because of Dr Brock?" I found this hard to credit. After all, she had been only a youngster, a far from normally raised teenager. With the best of intentions, she had tried to show her gratitude to the man who had saved her, in the only way she knew. What other gift did she have to offer? She had not understood him, but how could she? She came from a different world.

Again the look of amazement. "Dr Brock? What does he have to do with it? I knew from when I was a small kid I wasn't fit to live."

"What do you mean?"

"They showed us films at school, about Jews. Jews were compared to rats. They were not human, they were sub-human. Like vermin, they had to be destroyed."

"And you believed this?"

"Why shouldn't I? My schoolmates did. They wouldn't speak to me. They had been my friends for years."

"But surely you knew better?"

"Better than whom? These weren't street louts calling us names, this was Authority, this was the Government, they were State documentaries, shown compulsorily in all the schools, in all the cinemas.

"My father's friends saw them; professional people, lawyers, doctors, judges, even; people who knew us and people who didn't. Famous people, religious people, writers, everyone - no-one said it wasn't true. So I believed it. I knew I was fit only to die. When I didn't die, when I wasn't exterminated for being a Jew, I knew I had to punish myself."

"But afterwards, when you were grown up, you knew it was all filth and rubbish, it was madness, you couldn't have gone on thinking that way?"

"What you learn as a child is never unlearnt. We all believe it. Always."

It was at that point I realised that it was not just the delay in returning to Israel after Saoud died. It was *all* a punishment! After the Camps, the Sanatorium, into which she had found her inevitable way by deliberate starvation. And had she not chosen to come to Palestine by the hardest way, leading herself again into the prison of tuberculosis?

It was not through fear or hesitation that she had not gone to Hanita, that she had married a man she did not love and lived with him among an alien people to whom she could never belong.

She had not thought herself worthy. She had fought to leave Jordan, she had fought for her little girls, but never hard enough.

And when the way was at last wide open for her to leave, she had not done so.

She had lingered on, she had nursed a dying man who had no real need of her; even when he was dead, she had stayed on, alone, a domestic drudge among a hostile people, until she had no alternative but to go.

When she finally came back, had we not unwittingly thrust her into yet another prison, the companion of the Dying and the Dead? How fitting it had seemed to her! How readily she had accepted! Were there other choices? There are always choices.

But not for Rachel. I had thought I understood her, but I had not understood her at all. I had envisioned her a strong woman, determined to live the life 'she was meant to live', to be as she was, and it was this strength that attracted me. A woman who had gone through the Holocaust, and emerged untouched, undeviating in her determination to live her own Jewish life. This is what I had believed.

I, too, wanted to be like that. I wanted to be the Gerda who had *not* been witness to Tanta's suffering, who had *not* endured watching her loving mother's capacity for cruelty to her own mother, who had *not* been in terror of a brother's incestuous lust. I had so little will. I was like an obedient child. The waves washed over me, I drifted in their wake. Tanta made me uncertain. Evelyn's tastes dictated mine, Dr Lustig held me in a job I didn't like, Avi was taking me - at this point, I stopped, I didn't want to go any further.

But the Rachel who wanted to 'live as she was meant to be' was *not* the Rachel who would have been, had the Holocaust never happened. She had not given in, she had not accepted the sentence of death, she had fought for her life and succeeded; but she had *not* emerged unchanged.

The Holocaust was real, and the Rachel who survived encompassed also these realities. It made no difference that some of these realities were irrational.

Of course Rachel did not 'believe' that she was sub-human. But she acknowledged a guilt she did not accept rationally, as something conditioned into her. She expressed herself as a whole person - that was irrational in her as well as that which was not.

"What you learn as a child..." - had not all her childhood been a preparation for the Holocaust's dictate? 'Being Jewish' - something not quite nice, spoken of in hushed tones, like cancer or tuberculosis, or being a cripple. This was the way her parents had seen their Jewishness - as a handicap, a mark on the escutcheon, something to be suppressed, glossed over, till it became no more than an unimportant foible, like wearing unmatched socks. The step from condemnation by parental authority to condemnation by society was a small one. How could she not believe?

Rachel saw as her goal the expression of what she was, a Jewish woman, who belonged in Israel and had a part to play in its society. But the past was also in Rachel, a person bearing a burden of guilt, an undeserving person, who had evaded due punishment, and therefore must inflict it upon herself. It made no sense. But it was the lesson of the Holocaust, and the Holocaust had happened, and was in Rachel.

The woman who was 'meant to be' had the Holocaust not happened was entirely different. How would she have lived? A German matron, a wife who played cards and the piano, took her children to school and polished the furniture (maids were so careless!)? Who went discreetly - like her parents - to Synagogue on Yom Kippur; and then washed her hands of all this nonsense for another year? Who would she have married? Probably a non-Jew; a professional, perhaps a lawyer, or one of her father's up and coming young men? They would have two or three children, no more, polite, obedient and respectful German children who would never go to Synagogue at all.

Or would she have been snared, somehow, by the Great Adventure, seduced into polishing her shiny ideals, going as a young pioneer to Palestine, to live in a kibbutz? Would she have married a kibbutznik and had her own Jewish children? Would she have gone to Hanita, after all? Scenarios. Fantasies. Nothing more.

But what had this to do with me?

I had been brought up in my own country, I did not have this guilt. I was more like Avi than I was like Rachel - we had imbibed the same culture, the biggest difference between us was the barely hundred miles between Jerusalem and Haifa.

Why had I felt - did I still feel - that Rachel's life and mine were entangled, and in hers was a clue to the locked part in mine, that I needed so badly to open and explore? That Rachel could make me whole?

I had learnt nothing, save that Rachel's life now made sense. She was a strong woman who accepted what she had become, in its harsh entirety. Who did what she had to do, who made do with what she had. The life of a survivor.

Was this the message? That I, too, must live with what I had? I did not think so.

I felt only confusion.

I said to her: "I may not ever see you again."

She said nothing. Lips tight. Eyes without a spark.

"Don't you have any feelings for me?"

"Feelings? All I know about is tricks, scheming, using my head... Games you play for survival. If you had feelings you were dead."

She was back in Mauthausen. She had nothing for me. I was monstrously hurt.

But it was a lie. She had feelings, alright. After a time, her lower lip began to quiver. With an immense effort, she said the most unexpected thing.

"Break a leg, liebchen. Break a leg."

24. ISRAEL, 1979

Driving out of Jerusalem, on my way home to Tel Aviv, in Jerusalem's special golden glow as the sun was setting, it all came together for me at last. It was sudden and complete, truly like a revelation; and at what more appropriate time and place?

I was no longer that sweet child, Sheindele, the little girl who had pined for a pretty dress to wear at her sister's wedding, stopped there forever, in Tanta's darkening mind. I was not that child.

In Rachel's growing up, in which I had participated, from child to woman, Sheindele, too, had grown up, in me, just as she must have done in real life - married, no doubt, and had children of her own.

Sheindele and Rachel had not shared the same actual happenings. Moreover, Rachel had survived. Sheindele had vanished into the heart of the Holocaust; in what way she had met her end I did not know. Most probably, her bones and that of her children nourished that too green, that poisonously phosphorus green grass of Babi Yar.

But the essence was the same, the Holocaust was a single experience. Sheindele survived in Rachel and grew up in Rachel. She had therefore grown up in me; the childish part of me no longer dominated me, sapping my will and purpose, obedient to every adult command.

In the maturing of Sheindele I had not lost her, but I too had become a woman, a fully sexual woman who could respond to a loving man. Who was not moved by every shifting wind, who could 'be what I was meant to be'.

As well as Sheindele, Tanta was in me. Rachel was Tanta, just as she was also Sheindele.

These women who had not survived in life survived in Rachel, and in me. We all flowed into each other.

25. ISRAEL, 1979

I called my brother Uri, in Haifa.

"Gerda! What's up?"

"I'm getting married and going to live in Germany. This is to say goodbye."

A pause, longer than it should have been. "That's absolutely marvellous! Congratulations! When can you bring him over to meet us?"

"I can't. We're leaving on Sunday."

Another pause. Different.

"Perhaps we can come to the airport and see you off?"

"I don't think it would be a good idea. I'm quite a bit pregnant. I think the less fuss, the better."

Jaunty voice. "Well, lots of good luck all the same. Thanks for letting us know."

I had hurt him, of course. On purpose, even if without any conscious intention. It gave me no satisfaction. I would have liked to love him, but I couldn't.

The girls at the office made me a farewell party. It was happy and touching. They stroked my distended stomach "for luck" and gave me the ugliest cosmetics and toiletry kit (I don't use cosmetics) I have ever seen, plus a silver spoon for the baby. I kissed them all. In a year, I wouldn't remember their names.

Then I drove the Volkswagen over to my friendly garage owner who was going to put it up on blocks and wouldn't hear of payment and would sell it for me when I wrote. I was ready to go.

On the way to the airport, I made my last farewell to the country. Who would look after it while I was away? It, too was our child. I think Avi felt the same thing. Parenthood wouldn't be a novelty for us, we had been into it since we could remember.

26. MUNICH, 1979

It was a shock, I hadn't been prepared for it. The moment I got out of the airport at Munich, I hated Germany.

I had expected a feeling of distaste, a mild distress, but more that there would be specific things I wouldn't like, I would look for and find things to dislike, to complain about to Avi. Everything would be much more muted. I had not expected such violent feeling, nor that it would be so generalised. I loathed their busy faces, their language and their voices. I loathed the touch of my feet on their pavements. I didn't say a word.

We took a taxi to the hotel. All the time, I closed my eyes. Avi took my hand. In the hotel room, it was better, much better. Only the two of us. A sort of home.

They had given us a suite. There were television sets and phones in both rooms, and a bar and a dressing room as well as a separate bath and toilet.

I looked at Avi with a new respect.

"They certainly want you a lot."

"It's nothing. Just wait till the Mercedes pulls up."

It wasn't such a joke. They *had* bought him a car. The desk clerk called to say it was in the garage. We went down and looked at it. It wasn't a Mercedes, but it was a brand-new metallic finish Audi 80. I bowed low.

"Would you care to trample over me and get in, Master?"

He hugged me. "It's yours too, you know. All I have is yours."

Who could resist someone like that?

"I've got something that's yours, too."

"I know. Next year we'll make him some company." A future. Not to be sneezed at.

Because my feelings were so violent, perhaps they were transient. At least, I fought them, successfully, with the violence of my love for him. That evening there was a Get-Together Party. Mostly foreigners. The locals, Avi explained, would probably only turn up in the morning for the first working session.

The snacks were very substantial: smoked salmon on white bread and hot shrimps and caviare on toast in abundance. A rich country. We wouldn't need dinner that night.

I sampled. Agreeably, I said "hello", mostly, it seemed, to Americans. Avi had lost me. Something, I learned later, some specific metamorphosis that happened only at scientific meetings had taken place, turning the most attentive of husbands and lovers into completely neglectful talking machines, eagerly buttonholing total strangers to tell them about 'their work'.

I tried the white wine. The hearty air conditioning - it was a cool grey evening - dried the air and made me thirsty. It was a good wine and I drank rather a lot.

Eventually Avi, replete with intellectual fulfilment, found me. He had been drinking a bit, too.

We fell upon our bed, which was divided in the middle into two equal portions, each with a monstrous feather quilt. Someone had turned back the sheets and left a carefully wrapped chocolate mint on a piece of cardboard on each of our huge pillows. I thumped one. Down, of course.

We made love in one of the peculiar positions we had been using lately so as not to disturb our son.

"Move over, you bastard," said Avi, to my stomach, 'pretend' fiercely.

I giggled.

"There's nothing to laugh about. This isn't one of your spoilt Jewish brats. It's an Arab kid who knows respect. Father comes first."

I was drunker than I knew.

I began to sing "I belong to Glesca..." I must have heard it on some BBC World Service broadcast. Why it registered, I don't know.

"What's that?"

"Harry Lauder."

"Who's Harry Lauder?"

I told him.

The next morning, while we were gorging on the buffet breakfast - they certainly know how to bake bread, the rolls were delicious (rolls I thought, ovens, I thought) - Avi told me he would be occupied all day, till just before dinner-time. There were sessions, there was a poster display, a trade exhibition and people he had to see.

"Take the Audi," he said. "Go for a drive, see the countryside. Maybe one of the other women will join you. Do some shopping. Here." He handed me a small fortune in German marks.

Was this already a change in Avi? He never told me what to do. A German change? Rubbish, I thought, it's just we've never been on holiday together, at least, me on holiday while he works. He's just his usual caring self. I gave him an enthusiastic goodbye kiss. No-one could have noticed the element of doubt.

"Don't worry, I'll find plenty to do. I'll be back before you are."

"Buy me socks. Summer ones. Brown." Avi had a thing about socks. Different thicknesses for winter and summer. Different materials. Different colours. Different lengths.

I didn't take the Audi. I took a bus to the centre of town. It was a cool clear day, cloudy, but not with rain clouds. The centre was all shops and walkways and there was the famous clock. The violent hatred wasn't in me any more, or at least not consciously. I didn't feel anything at all.

The clock chimed ten o'clock and I stood for the requisite five or ten minutes and watched the stilted figures in the medieval costumes just above the clock face as they moved in their appointed ways.

Then I went into Kaufhof and bought Avi twenty pairs of different socks, an extravagant array. I didn't buy anything else, except a cup of coffee, which I took to a bench on the street. The sun was out. Bombed Munich, rebuilt, looked rich and modern. Many shoppers. A man sat down beside me, an elderly man. Maybe a widower, good pension, didn't like sitting at home, went out and bought himself the necessary rubbish, a bit of tobacco, a new pipe, a couple of handkerchiefs. Mostly just to be with people, to have something to do.

A small list on the refrigerator door, which he added to every night. Repair radio, sugar, corn flakes, navy-blue socks ... He said, "Guten Tag."

"I'm sorry, I don't speak German. I'm a foreigner." I wanted to speak to him.

"English? Do you speak English?"

"I speak English but I don't come from there. I'm an Israeli," I said.

"Actually, I am half Swiss. I was in Switzerland during the War."

I spoke to a lot of people. I sought out the older ones, the ones who had been youngsters, then, but I spoke to young people too. I spent the whole day, just sitting on that bench. There weren't many benches with free places, I always had company. I even bought my lunch at a stall, a huge long sausage in a bread roll, and talked to people as I ate.

"How was your day?" asked Avi, when he came in. It was almost dinner-time. He was flushed and excited. His had been good. He wanted to have a quick dinner and do a bit of last minute work on his talk, which would be in tomorrow's afternoon session. He wanted to check his slides.

"I talked to a lot of people."

"Oh?" He was far away.

"I've found out a new shattering truth," I told him. "There aren't any Germans. The whole thing's a myth! Any old ones, anyway."

"What do you mean?"

"I sat for six hours in the centre of Munich and I talked to about twelve men and women, I guess over sixty years of age. There wasn't a German among them. There were half Austrians and half Italians and quarter Swedes, and Norwegians, you name it. There weren't any real Germans at all. There weren't any Nazis. Nobody did anything to anybody. There wasn't any War. There were only those half-something-also people, and they either didn't know anything, they all lived in inaccessible places in the mountains, or they weren't in Germany at all. It didn't exist. The country arose, apparently, by spontaneous combustion, around 1946. Before that, there was the Weimar Republic. There wasn't anything in between, at all. There was a time warp. Or a black hole."

I had encountered one woman in a public lavatory. I asked her for change, it was a pay toilet.

She said: "Where are you from?" She didn't know my accent.

"Israel."

"Ach mein Gott! Mein Mann ist nicht in der SS gewesen!"

Like hell he wasn't! It was as good as a confession.

She said it as if she had learnt it by rote.

I looked at the twenty pfennig coin she was handing me, opened my bag, took out a twenty DM note and crushed it into her hand.

"Ah nein! Das ist zu viel."

But it wasn't. It wasn't nearly enough. Nothing could ever be enough.

"The other side also was not always 'in ordnung!'
You bombed Dresden! You destroyed it! A civilian city!"

It was where the SS sent their wives and children. Their women wore necklaces made of other dead women's gold teeth.

"Aber Dresden! Es war so schön!"

Not more beautiful than a Jewish child.

Avi said, "Can you blame them? Talking to an Israeli."

"Oh yes, I can blame them!" The violent reaction flooded over me. I said: "Go on, you're dying to! Say it!"

"O.K. It's true. I don't understand. Why is it different? Why is it different for the fucking Jews? What's so special about the Holocaust? The Armenians got massacred by the million, they don't go on and on about it. They don't forget, but it isn't part of their fucking daily lives, one, two generations after. How about the Cambodians? That wasn't genocide? The Kurds?

"I'm perfectly willing to admit the Jews are the Big Mac when it comes to suffering, nobody wants to take it away from them, but can't you let it rest? For Chrissake, it was forty years ago! You weren't there! You were hardly born! Why is it different from all the other killing sprees that happened, that are happening all the time?"

"It was different." I didn't know how to express it so I stopped for a moment. Then I went on. "Not for the Jews. They were slaughtered and mourn their dead. That's natural. It was different for the Germans. Always, in what you call the 'killing sprees', it was done in hot blood. There was always passion: virgins were sacrificed in terror of powerful gods; fear dictated the burning of witches, fear, or love, or hate. In despair, in vengeance, for hunger, for greed, in anger; maybe just a pure animal lust for killing. Primeval man, an animal out of control.

"Not thinking, rational man, builders of society, societies that expressed the subjugation of the animal within, that made laws for rational man.

"The Holocaust was perpetrated in cold blood. By men planning a new social order. Administrators, scientists and engineers, diligent, educated men who designed the tools, the ovens and the chemicals, the railway timetables, to kill in the most up to-date, cost-efficient way, six million of their fellow men. It was their daily work. A part of their normal daily life.

"They were not animals crazed by passion. They were businessmen. Pedantic men, interested in doing a good job, in creating an industry, in 'optimising' the 'product'. The 'product' was death. They thought about efficient utilisation of by-products - the spectacles, the fat, the teeth, the hair. How to avoid time-wasting protest by the 'human material'. How to get rid of the waste. Cultured, thoughtful men, specialists, technicians, who went home to their wives and kids after a hard day's work, who listened to Beethoven, took the dog for a walk, helped with the shopping and the chores. Decent men. Homo sapiens. Rational Man.

"This never happened before. It has changed us all. It divides us into two groups. Those who were touched by the Holocaust; and then there are all the rest."

I said, "Do you know what they called it, officially, in all the documents, all the discussions? 'Vernichtung'. To make people into nothing. That's what's happening to me here."

He didn't say anything. What could he say? After a long time, a long silence:

"I could never have done anything like that."

I hadn't even thought it.

I said, "I know."

Did I know? Could anyone ever know?

The invisible numbers on my wrist were neither a mark of honour nor achievement. They just were. They signified only a difference, like when a new class arises in the process of evolution, a group of individuals sufficiently different from the others to be recognised as a class. The edges might be blurred, it might not be possible to identify any individual with certainty. But the class was distinct. Holocaust Man.

I stood on my side of this Divide, and Avi on the other.

Not all the wars of the Jews and Arabs could have separated us. But the Holocaust did.

27. MUNICH, 1979

At dinner, I told Avi about the younger people.

"They didn't know, either. That period just got wiped out of the school curriculum. They were never told. Of course, they all learned about it afterwards, but they're still convinced 'their' parents didn't do anything, didn't know anything about the extermination of the Jews. They feel a certain remorse. They're especially interested in Israel. They want to do penance. They nearly all want to come for a year and work in a kibbutz. But it's nothing personal. Their families weren't part of it. They've spoken to their parents about it and they believe them.

"It was always someone else - the louts, the duped fascist youths, the illiterate, the uneducated, the ignorant working class; only never them."

"They're all like that?"

"Not all. There was the 'pardon, Meine gnadige Frau, but the Jews deserved what they got, they weren't like you. They were rats eating away at our country. The gang of Jews at the trough, the international conspiracy, the control of the press - you name it."

"Many?"

"No. Only one. And there was the opposite, too. A doctor, oncologist, thirty, thirty-five perhaps. He said his curiosity was aroused by the fact that history in school stopped in 1930. When he was sixteen, he took a train and went to Bergen-Belsen, he spoke to people in the nearby village. 'Of course we all knew,' they told him, 'You could smell it for miles.' He spoke to a journalist. 'Everybody knew,' he said, 'You couldn't help knowing. There were thousands of soldiers who had done guard duty at the Camps, there were eye-witnesses everywhere. There wasn't anybody who didn't know. My father was a fascist,' he said, 'He was an SS man.' He was the only person I spoke to whose father was a German and a Nazi. I asked him what his relationship was with his father, and he said, "Thank God he's dead'."

That night, I went totally irrational. I didn't want to sleep in the bed. I said I would sleep on the floor.

"For Christ's sake, why?"

"The mattress could be made of hair. My great-grandmother's hair."

"The bloody mattress isn't made of hair! No one makes mattresses of hair nowadays. It's fucking made of fucking foam rubber!"

Avi didn't often lose his cool. He tore the ticking off a mattress cover and showed me. It was foam rubber. I slept on the bed.

But the next morning, I felt better. I went out, and did some real shopping and hardly spoke to anyone. The pavements under my feet weren't blood any more. It was just a place.

I thought, with a kind of amazement, "You get used to it. You can get used to anything." I knew this was not true. But I wanted it to be.

That night I told Avi: "I think it's going to be alright."

But two hours later, I was into the nightmares. Some of them were monolithic. We were having the buffet breakfast, for example, Avi and I, but when I looked up, the waiters behind the long tables were SS guards, with the silver eagle's wings, and whips, and guard dogs, and we were surrounded by barbed wire.

Others were more insidious. I went to school to fetch home my little boy. He was called Dieter. He called me 'Mutti' and he told me he loved his 'Herr Papa' and would obey him always. He had short blond hair and wore knickerbockers and when he greeted me he said, "Grüss Gott". He told me he was going to be the 'Spirit of Germany' in the class play, he would wear a uniform and shout 'Arbeit Macht Frei'. He made me sick, I hated the sight of him. "What have they done with my son?' I shouted, "You aren't my son."

Avi comforted me. In his own way. "Don't you worry," he said, "we'll bring him up to be a proper little Arab terrorist, Kalashnikov rifle and all. He won't know one end from the other. We won't let him shave, just like Arafat. They'll capture him and put him in the prison at Tel Mond and we'll send him postcards.

"He'll come out after twenty years and marry a Jewish girl from Tel Aviv just like his dad."

No-one else could have made me laugh at such dreams. I clung to him. I don't know how, but I knew my Armageddon was on its sure way.

In the morning, Avi said, "I think I know what's wrong. You think you're Panorama." We had often seen BBC Panorama programmes, on the "Second Look" on Israeli television. It came after the nine o'clock news. "You've made yourself into a fucking investigative reporter. 'And now folks, Germany Today. As seen through Israeli eyes'. Da da da and so on. For Christ's sake, all you've got to do is buy socks from those people, not study their inner thoughts. Did you go about doing that back home? Did you ask the greengrocer, 'Cheating on the Income Tax lately? How do you feel about capital punishment?' You fucking well didn't. You said: 'Kilo of potatoes, please and make sure they're all sound.' You didn't care what was on his conscience and whether he slept at night. You didn't make a survey of Tel Avivians in the street and what they thought about the starving Ethiopians.

"Your friends were your friends, that was different. Leave the bloody strangers alone! What the hell do you care whether the telephone repair man's a nice guy or not?

"Just care about me. Care about the boy. You can call him Judah the Maccabee, if you want.

"We'll make friends. They'll be from a crowd like this, the people at this Conference - intelligent, interesting people, scientists and their wives; they'll probably be more humanist than we are. These are the people you'll live with, not the man in the street. People like your oncologist. He was different, wasn't he?

"Gerda, do me a favour. Don't go off on your own tomorrow. Go on the Accompanying Persons' Trip; with our kind of people."

"Where is it to?"

"Just the job for you. Visits to stately homes. Lovely furniture, china. Lots of antiques."

He knew I loved antiques.

It's a frustrating passion in Israel, where everything is either very new (last hundred years), or very old indeed, too old, back to the birth of Christ and way beyond; coins, lamps, perfume bottles, bits of glass, all in the rich collector range. You could never pick up an unrecognised bargain, a flow-blue plate, a Georgian finger bowl, from among the junk. There were just a few 'antique' shops, European style, but they sold really junk - 1940's furniture, all brown sauce and varnish, Woolworth earthenware tea sets; and so on.

"But I won't be able to buy anything. All I could do is look."

"Exactly!"

28. MUNICH - TEL-AVIV, 1979

The bus wasn't full, there were only about thirty people in it. Twenty-six were women, presumably wives, and one was a male 'accompanying person, all distinguished by their orange badges. There were three genuine participants with their white badges, playing hooky - two young, maybe newly-marrieds wanting to spend time with their wives, and one older man, who had heard it all before, top of his field and nowhere further to go, didn't need to listen to lectures any more. At a certain point even scientists stop caring. Most of the people were locals from other German towns.

I looked for anyone who was obviously an English-speaker among the ladies sitting alone. Americans generally wore a lot of make up. The English wore skirts and plain blouses and even pearls. I picked one lady with an intelligent, alert face and lipstick and plucked eyebrows.

"May I join you?"

"Pardon? Oh, certainement, oui!"

She was Belgian, and a Flemish speaker at that. She did know a bit of English, but conversation soon ran out.

Once we were out of Munich, and in the open countryside, I was interested in the scenery. That wood, was it big enough for them to have hidden in? Could they have dug a pit or found a cave, coming out only at night to pick cabbages and potatoes from the fields? Were the villages too near, so they might have been spotted by someone driving back late from Munich, or did the villagers hunt for rabbits at night?

What happened after a year or so, when their underwear was filthy and smelly and began to fall off in shreds? Could you bathe in the river? How would they cope with children, with finding food in the winter snow? If you were a woman who menstruated, how did you manage without pads? Could you have survived at all, or only with the help of a villager, and how did you know whom, if any, it was safe to ask? What kind of person could come out of such an experience, muscles wasted, eyes hardly able to see in the light? Were there descendants of these tragedies who didn't know it was all over, pale creatures, half worm, half people, still living in caves?

It wasn't exactly your normal tourist reaction.

When I thought about it, I realised that I related to these experiences, not as if they had happened to some unknown person, not even Sheindele, not Rachel, but as if they had happened, or were happening, to me.

We stopped for coffee at one of these vast café-cum-tourist shops, where there were hundreds of artefacts on display, things no sensible person would think of acquiring at home. Badly sewn purses in bad leather, with a stamped picture of a mountain and a 'present from Bavaria' lettered onto them. Factory-made wooden animals. Pen trays. Key-rings with furry animals, poor screen-printed scarves and table mats and the like; they weren't 'Presents' from Bavaria, they were highly over-priced. I didn't buy anything, I drank good coffee instead, but many of the other women did. Their friends back home were different. I couldn't imagine presenting Rachel or Dr Lustig with a present from Bavaria. But then, I reminded myself, I was here to stay. I didn't have to buy anything at all for the people back home.

This came as a blow.

After the coffee break, we drove on. We arrived at an imposing Manor House. It wasn't particularly beautiful, but the setting was. Rolling mountains as a backdrop, a fine garden, then neat green fields.

Could they have survived in the mountains?

The furnishings in the public rooms of the house were exquisite. There were pieces - an ormolu clock, a Chinese mother-of-pearl inlaid cabinet - I would have killed for. Well, not killed. What was less pleasing was that there was so much of it. Every room was full of furniture, every surface had its ornaments, not one, but at least three or four. It was not a tasteful house. It was ready for the auction. I was suspicious - was it filled with loot, with spoil from Jewish homes? Perhaps the private rooms were less cluttered.

The 'family', in the shape of a shapely Countess, showed us around. It had been specially arranged. We were distinguished academics, not a 'regular' tour. Not Japanese with cameras, Germans on holiday with kids. She explained to us that all the German aristocracy were related through intermarriage with a single top family - which was half Danish, of course.

The Manor 'did' lunches. Ours was excellent: not heavy, asparagus soup, ham and cheese and the delicious bread and rolls. Ice cream, coffee and a good Moselle wine.

We had one other great House to visit, and then back to Munich. It was a well arranged tour. Leisurely; not too much driving, yet enough to feel out in the country, not too much tramping around. The guides, two of them, who were with us to look after us and count us and bring us safely home, were elderly ladies. Pin money. Too small a pension, or just something to get them out of the house.

The second House was much bigger. The furnishings were of an older period and looked as if they belonged. Our host was a middle-aged man who spoke perfect English. He too told us immediately that he was half-Danish. I chided myself. Perhaps they all were.

There was one beautiful room after another, all in much better harmony and taste. The last was the prize exhibit, a bedroom with all its original early eighteenth century furnishings, sheets, embroidered bedspread, commode and all.

'Leonard Bernstein slept in this bed. When he conducted the Munich orchestra he stayed here,' our host told us.

He didn't tell us whether Herman Goering had slept there too. Maybe he hadn't.

The tapestry behind and above the huge four-poster bed told a story. It was about one of his ancestors.

"The daughter wanted to marry a young man. The Count didn't think he was suitable, so the Count asked his friend, a Jew, (and there he was, in his skull-cap and caftan) to speak to the girl. He did, but she wouldn't listen - she ran away and married her lover. There they are, with the priest, being married. But it wasn't a success, as you see, in the end, they are sitting far apart, in separate chairs, and quite symbolically, the cat and the dog lie between them."

"And the Jew got all the money."

This came from the male 'accompanying person'. He was a German, from Heidelberg, an elderly man. There was a polite nervous titter. The Count began to speak again.

I heard an interrupting voice, a belligerent, hoarse voice I did not recognise, loud, rough and strong. It was mine.

"What's your problem?" I asked. "Didn't you get your elbows deep enough into Jewish blood? Didn't they give you enough of the loot? Didn't you get your share of the houses, the land, the furniture, the jewellery? Did they do you out of the gold teeth for a necklace for your wife? What's bothering you?"

"You animal," I said. "You disgusting animal. How dare you? On this soil, soaked with Jewish blood."

He sat down on a chair. He was embarrassed, but he wasn't more than embarrassed. The Jews were so touchy. After all, what had he said? Everyone knew the Jews liked money.

My voice went back to normal but I wasn't quite finished. I said: "I won't travel in the same bus with that animal!" I turned to the guide. "What are you going to do about it?"

It was much to be regretted, of course. People shouldn't really say, such things (out loud?). But it had nothing to do with them. They weren't responsible. They were only the guides.

They had lived next door to Dachau.

It was a phrase they knew. It was so expectable, it was like a caricature of themselves.

I asked the half-Danish aristocrat, who had so pointedly, so proudly hosted Leonard Bernstein, "Do you think you could call me a taxi?" He was glad to get away.

An American woman came up to me, then a second. We seemed to split into two groups - I and the Americans in one, the Germans and other Europeans on the other side, with the guides. One of them said, "Ladies and gentlemen, the visit is over. We must go back to the bus now." Their 'side' trouped off. The Americans stayed with me.

Our host returned. "Your taxi will be here in five minutes. I don't know how to apologise." He was distressed.

He was not ransomed. It was genuine distress, but it came too late. It should have happened when the words were spoken. They were spoken in his house.

We didn't talk much, on the way back to Munich, the American ladies and I. Small exchanges. "Have you enough room?" "I can easily move up." "At what hotel do you want to be dropped?" They didn't let me pay for the taxi. "But it was I who asked for it!" "We're all in this together." I let them have their share.

At the Intercontinental, I took my key and a message from Avi from the desk and went up to our room. I immediately phoned El Al. There was no place on the plane leaving from Munich the next day, but they could get me on the noon plane from Frankfurt to Tel Aviv, with a good connecting flight. "Did I want it?" I said "Yes", and gave them my name. "Miss or Mrs?" I said "Miss, and I'm pregnant." "How many months, Madam?" Discreet. "Six." "Oh, that'll be alright."

Avi's note simply said he had a meeting after the last session and might not be back till about eight. I pulled out my suitcase and began to pack. I had brought very little. Nearly all my clothes, my personal possessions, had been crated. Evelyn was supposed to send them off the moment I wrote that I was settled.

It didn't take me long. Then I sat down on the bed and waited for Avi. I had no tears. I was anger and ice.

He came in well before eight. He looked tired. He said, "Hello, how did it go? Hope you had a good day." Then he saw my face.

He saw the packed suitcase, near the door. "So this is it," he said, "just like that." I put my arms round him, but he didn't move.

I told him all about it, including the troglodytes and the blameless keep-us-out-of-it guides. I tried to explain to him what was still too new in me to be able to put in words easily, yet was so definite, so clear. I couldn't live in Germany, I told him, not because of the Germans. Because of me. A Gerda that stayed in Germany would be a bitter, hating woman, of no use to him, to her child, no use to herself. She would not be me. She would not be able to live the life that she was meant to lead. Introverted, suspicious, a battleground, she would be torn apart. It wasn't that he meant less to me than the sacrifice of living in Germany. I literally could not do it. It would be some other person, not me, not the someone he loved.

He sat down. He was white, and he was angry, too. "Do you think it is so easy for me? I've just had a drink with two men I'll be working in the same lab with, who knows? - maybe for the rest of my life, I've had lunch with them and coffee, I've spent hours with them and it's still 'Yes, Herr Direktor Meir' and 'No, Herr Elektronische Engineer Hockstein.' It will probably never be Avi and Otto and Hans unless I go to a Bierhalle with them and get disgustingly drunk and piss all over the place, then we'll be jolly good pals. Until the next day.

"They keep telling me how wonderful it will be after the snow falls; all the great ski-ing places. Herr Meir has a little kid of three, already skis like a champ.

"I'm a Mediterranean man. I like the sun. I can't stand the cold, mountains don't mean anything to me. I don't want to put on a pair of great fucking sticks and shove off and break both my legs. I want to lie half-naked on the beach at Tel Aviv and watch all the topless girls go by - only looking, mind you - the religious gnashing their teeth, the young girls 'pretend' lowering their eyes. I want to hear the sound of kids playing with their wooden bats and the celluloid balls, I want a ball to fall on me and bellow "Fuck off, you little bastards!" and hear their cheeky, "Fuck off, yourself!"

"I want you, I want the kid. You think I like it so much here? I want the pavement cafés and the young wide boys sitting there making their fabulous hundred dollar deals. I want the sun and the people and the noise."

"Oh Avi," I said miserably, "I know."

There wasn't that much difference between us. He couldn't live in Israel. He couldn't be a teacher - or a waiter - just to please me, to be with me and the child. His work was a big part of his life. Without it, he would also become a bitter, hating person, not the man I was used to, that I wanted and loved, the man who had already sacrificed something of himself at that altar and couldn't be expected to sacrifice more. Anyway, all this was theoretical. He could never go back now. They might go easy on him, he had done no harm, but there would have to be an example. A couple of years, maybe, in one of the better jails.

He said, "We could be together in the vacations. We could spend them in France or somewhere. Italy would be nice."

It would, but it couldn't last. He was a warm, loving man. He was a natural person, he would spend his evenings in the lab for a time, but, for how much time? A year? Some months? Someone was bound to come along, he was nice, he was handsome, he had a house with four bedrooms, they'd come crawling out of the woods. A 'Berthe', or an 'Ulrike', a 'Brunhilde' or what-have-you, with pretty yellow hair, trained to make a man happy, trained by mothers who had been brought up on 'Kinder, Kuche, Kirche'.

How could he resist that, a stranger in a strange country who didn't belong any more to a woman in a place he could never even visit?

Given the chance, would I not do the same?

The only real difference was my chances were so near nil. A woman of forty (soon), as Evelyn had said, with another man's kid. Who would want me? One look at these topless beauties, these long-legged black-haired girls, brimming with health and yoghurt..... If you fall easy, keep away!

He said, "I'll take you to the airport. Better get some sleep."

We lay, frantically entwined, till daybreak. We didn't speak. We had said it all.

He drove me to the airport, the next morning. He said, "You're early. You don't need to look at your wrist watch all the time."

I wasn't wearing a wrist watch.

He saw me on to the plane to Frankfurt. We both said there would never be anyone else and we would write. Like the Humphrey Bogart - Ingrid Bergman movie. "Here's looking at you, kid." Unreal.

I went through the special procedures for passengers on Israel-bound planes. I was surrounded by triumphant Israelis, displaying their kills - woollens and household wares and linen, probably made in Israel anyway, but at half the local price - if you don't count the taxes, the plane fare, the hotels and the rest.

I got on to the plane, and, eventually, when everyone sorted themselves out, and their guilty excess of hand luggage was tucked away, we took off. I unbuckled my belt, a special long one for pregnant women and overweight passengers, but still uncomfortably tight. I was not conscious of time passing. I didn't make plans.

I did not want to think, so I put on the earphones and listened to Bach. But thoughts kept obtruding. Images, too.

Avi's face as we parted at the barrier; he was losing his woman and child as inexorably as if he saw the metal doors of the gas chamber clanging behind us. Did this make him, too, a victim of the Holocaust, just as surely as I? If so, why did he see no number on his wrist? Was everyone, to some degree of extension, a victim? Or a murderer? Could one be both?

Was it only a matter of being aware, a technicality? From now on, would Avi, too, feel the pricks on his flesh?

Into my mind, underneath all my thoughts, a word was drifting. "Vernichtung!" To 'make into nothing'. To erase.

A blow to the heart of survival. We all struggled to survive, it was our very purpose, the blind drive of evolution itself. If not in ourselves, in others. To make our own particular mark upon the world, to ensure it would be carried onward and endure.

In Hebrew, a language not rich in curses, the most terrible one, hardly ever used, was "May your name be forgotten!" The Bible, too. Long lists of who begat who. Names.

'*Vernichtung*': To become nothing more than a blob of Tippex on history's recorded page.

The Holocaust, like landing on the moon, - had been 'one giant step for Man'; neither forward nor backward, but recognisably a step, leading in a new direction, a twist in evolution. Holocaust Man.

But the Holocaust had *not* succeeded in blotting out individuals, let alone a whole people. Tanta, when she gave up, when she turned her face to the wall, had she not done so with the knowledge that she, *and also Sheindele*, lived on in me?

Rachel, too. She had lifted her skirts to Dr Brock, she had killed for two potatoes and a moment of rest, but she had not turned herself into either a murderer or a whore. She had remained herself.

Here, another thought intruded. Rachel had described her long years at the hospital in Hebron as a self-imposed 'punishment'. But was it not also a fulfilment? I had not had the heart to tell her so, but the Hanita of 1948 was not the kibbutz of her dreams, perhaps of stories told to her by her grandmother of other, older kibbutzim, like Degania, or Ain Harod. The back-breaking toil, the hunger, the T.B. and malaria, the triumph over the reluctant soil, the euphoria, the singing and the dancing all night long - that belonged to an earlier time; in 1948 it was all over. Hanita, a relative latecomer, was already becoming prosperous. Neat huts had replaced the leaky tents. The comrades worked hard and ate stodgy, uninteresting and not very plentiful food. But malaria had gone, they were not sick, they already had a well-built dining room. People kept gardens. Water came out of a tap.

Had she not known this herself? Rachel had few illusions.

The years as a skivvy, doing the most menial of jobs, the long working hours, the physical exhaustion, the poor food - had Rachel seen this not only as a punishment but also as a realisation of her dream - to suffer, to sacrifice, to remain a Jew; to continue to grow and nurture her being on even this, the most unpromising, the most bitter of soils? Questions. Complexities within complexities. I knew I would turn them over, poke and prod, for the rest of my life.

At the back of my mind, I knew it would all turn out alright. Dr Lustig would find me a job. Rachel would be there, a part of me. And Evelyn, trustworthy Evelyn, would take me into her charge. Would provide money, infant clothes, a home for as long as I needed it; would go with me to the hospital and visit me and take me and my son out of there in due time. Would do my baby-sitting and give me her sound and useful advice.

There were day nurseries for my son and theatres and movies and concerts and pubs for singles like me. A life without Avi - that was why I kept it there, at the back of my mind. Not happiness, but a way I could live as the person I was meant to be. My life. My grown up life.

When the captain announced that we were landing, I fastened my seat belt. When the plane sets down at Ben Gurion airport, Israelis always clap - whether because the Captain has landed it well and safely, or whether because of the joy that they had overcome all dangers, traversed the perilous jungles of Marks & Spencer's and Kaufhof and Le Printemps and returned home safe at last - I never knew. It always made me feel superior, because it was so naïve.

But this time, as the wheels bounced on the tarmac, I, too, clapped like an idiot with all the rest.